THE TOUCH OF LOVE

Book of Love, Book Two

Meara Platt

Text by Meara Platt
Cover by Dar Albert

Dragonblade Publishing, Inc. is an imprint of Kathryn Le Veque Novels, Inc.
P.O. Box 23
Moreno Valley, CA 92556
ceo@dragonbladepublishing.com

Produced in the United States of America

First Edition 2019
Trade Paperback Edition

Dearest Reader;

Thank you for your support of a small press. At Dragonblade Publishing, we strive to bring you the highest quality Historical Romance from the some of the best authors in the business. Without your support, there is no 'us', so we sincerely hope you adore these stories and find some new favorite authors along the way.

Happy Reading!

CEO, Dragonblade Publishing

Additional Dragonblade books by Author Meara Platt

The Moonstone Landing Series
Moonstone Landing (novella)
Moonstone Angel (novella)
The Moonstone Duke
The Moonstone Marquess
The Moonstone Major

The Book of Love Series
The Look of Love
The Touch of Love
The Taste of Love
The Song of Love
The Scent of Love
The Kiss of Love
The Chance of Love
The Gift of Love
The Heart of Love
The Hope of Love (novella)
The Promise of Love
The Wonder of Love
The Journey of Love
The Dream of Love (novella)
The Treasure of Love
The Dance of Love
The Miracle of Love
The Remembrance of Love (novella)

Dark Gardens Series
Garden of Shadows
Garden of Light
Garden of Dragons

Garden of Destiny
Garden of Angels

The Farthingale Series
If You Wished For Me (A Novella)

The Lyon's Den Series
Kiss of the Lyon
The Lyon's Surprise
Lyon in the Rough

Pirates of Britannia Series
Pearls of Fire

De Wolfe Pack: The Series
Nobody's Angel
Kiss an Angel
Bhrodi's Angel

Also from Meara Platt
Aislin
All I Want for Christmas

To all who are noble at heart

CHAPTER ONE

Wellesford, England
August 1815

"HEAVEN HELP ALL bachelors," Nathaniel Sherbourne, Earl of Welles, said to his companions as they stared out the window of his study at the three young ladies seated on a fallen log beside the Sherbourne Manor pond. Despite the heat of the August sun, their bonnets had been tossed aside on the grassy bank and their heads were bowed over a book. "Beast, your wife has just handed *The Book of Love* to Poppy."

Alexander Beastling, Duke of Hartford, shook his head and laughed. He looked quite the pirate with a black eyepatch over the eye he'd lost during the Napoleonic War. "Are you quaking in your boots, Nathaniel?"

"Should I be? They're handling the blasted thing as though it's Merlin's mythical book of spells just recovered after a thousand years buried in the earth."

Their third companion, Thaddius MacLauren, Laird of Caithness, had been quietly staring at the young ladies, but now spoke. "The lasses believe it contains a powerful magic. After all, Beast was the bachelor who could not be taken down. But look at him now, not only married, but besotted and deeply in love with Goose."

Nathaniel frowned. "Thad, what are you thinking? The book had nothing to do with it."

His friend shrugged. "Och, but what if it did? You and I will be in deep trouble, my friend. We like to think we have control over our own destinies, but that book could prove us wrong." He ran a hand across the back of his neck. "Lord, it's hot. My throat is parched. I'm going to walk to Wellesford for a drink. Care to join me in a pint of ale, Beast?"

"What about me?" Nathaniel frowned once more. "Am I to face Poppy alone? Not that I'm afraid of the girl. She's pretty, of course. Who wouldn't be enchanted by those big, blue eyes and dark curls? But she's like a sister to me. I've known her for most of my life."

"Death knell," Beast teased. "They're conspiring to make you Poppy's test frog. I was Goose's, and look where it got me."

Nathaniel folded his arms across his chest. "I'm up for the challenge. As I said, I've known her forever. I'm not going to fall for her simply because you fell hard and fast for your wife." Besides, he had bigger problems on his mind and wasn't about to add Poppy Farthingale to his already thorny complications.

Thad returned his gaze to the pond. "Ye'd better not fall in love with Poppy, or I'll be doomed. That would leave me with your sister, and you know how much Loopy hates me."

Nathaniel sighed. "She doesn't hate you. At least, she wouldn't if you stopped provoking her at every turn. Calling her Penelope instead of Loopy would help, for starters."

Thad grinned. "But where's the fun in that? Besides, Beast never called Olivia by her given name. She's always been Goose to him, and she has never minded. Bollocks, they're looking this way. They're coming for you, Nathaniel." He slapped his friend on the shoulder. "Come on, Beast. Let's head to the Golden Hart before they spot us. We'll go out the back way."

They both cast Nathaniel parting grins as they strode to the door.

"Cowards," he called after them. "You can't leave me alone with the three of them."

"Join us afterward. We'll save you a pint." Beast was unable to stifle his mirth. "Assuming you survive Poppy's first onslaught."

"The girl is harmless and I'll prove it to you. I'll prove it to all of you," he shouted after his friends who were deserting him like rats on a sinking ship. "Blast it," he muttered after they'd left. "She's never been kissed. And she thinks to seduce me? Hah! I'll show you all."

Nathaniel strode into the entry hall and casually leaned his hip against the elegant table that stood in its center. He folded his arms across his chest and fixed his expression to appear bored and unaffected.

"Good morning, Nathaniel," his sister said, walking into the house with her bonnet in hand and an irritating smirk on her face.

Beast's wife, Olivia, cast him a similar smirk. He bowed his head to acknowledge her presence. "Morning, Goose."

"Is my husband still here or has he fled to Wellesford?" She was so cheerful, she practically chirped.

He arched an eyebrow. "He's fled to town with Thad."

She shook her head of ginger curls and sighed. "The cowards. Come on, Penelope. Let's go find them. Poppy, will you come with us? Leave the book upstairs. It's too valuable to tote around town."

"Yes, I'd love to. I hear Captain Gordon is visiting Lord and Lady Plimpton again. I hope we run into him. I'd love to hear more about his adventures." She hurried upstairs without so much as a nod in Nathaniel's direction.

He turned to scowl at his sister. "When did Poppy meet Plimpton's nephew?"

"Last month and again at Olivia and Beast's wedding last week." She rolled her eyes as though Andrew Gordon's arrival was something he ought to have noticed. "Don't you remember him? You hosted their breakfast and invited everyone in Wellesford to attend. He looked quite dashing in his regimentals. Why are you surprised that Poppy is eager to see him? He danced two dances with her and couldn't take his eyes off her the entire day."

"Gordon is a horse's arse. She can't seriously choose him as the man she wishes to marry."

"And why not?" Penelope tipped her chin up in that irritatingly indignant manner she'd perfected. "Do you have a better man to suggest? Such as yourself, perhaps?"

"Put the absurd notion out of your head at once."

"Then why are you so put out? You ought to be relieved that she has no interest in you. So you needn't worry that we'll interfere with your courtship of that… of Charlotte Winthrow."

"Lady Charlotte will arrive at the end of the week with her father." He clenched his teeth to stem his annoyance, knowing his sister was purposely goading him. "Be nice to her. She isn't a dimwit."

"I never said she was."

"You implied it with that look." He said no more as Poppy came bounding down the stairs, her steps light and carefree.

"I'm ready." Her cheeks were pink from rushing to drop off the book in her bedchamber and hurrying back to her friends. Perhaps they were also pink from her time spent in the sunshine. Her gown was a pale blue confection that looked quite fetching on her and brought out the crystal blue of her eyes and the lushness of her long, dark hair that was loosely pinned up at the moment.

Not that he was looking at Poppy or suddenly noticing anything about her.

Certainly not her lips.

Or that they were slightly pouty and her lower lip had a nice, plump fullness that would make kissing them quite pleasant.

He shook off the thought.

She was merely his sister's friend.

Poppy finally deigned to acknowledge him, casting him a warmhearted smile. "Will you join us, Nathaniel?"

Is it a trick question? Was she about to test one of the spells she'd read in *The Book of Love* on him? Why was she smiling at him? No matter. He was ready to meet the challenge. "Yes, I think I will."

Poppy cast him another sweet smile and continued out the door.

In truth, she'd always been a pleasant girl, but she was now in possession of this book and he feared it would turn her into… what? *An irresistible siren? A dangerous seductress?* Hardly likely since the girl had no experience whatsoever.

Did she understand the first thing about men?

He doubted it.

Not that he cared one way or the other, but she was a guest in his home and it was his duty to make certain she did not get into trouble. Right now, he had enough on his mind and did not need Poppy's attempts to find love compounding his worries.

There was nothing he could do about the other concern at the moment. But *The Book of Love* in innocent hands was dangerous, and Poppy was still an innocent.

He fully intended to keep her that way. Andrew Gordon was not going to get his lecherous hands on her.

"Why are you frowning?" his sister asked, falling back to walk beside him as they strolled along the shaded hedgerow paths toward Wellesford. Goose and Poppy had run ahead, leaving them out of earshot for the moment, which was a good thing. He had plenty to say to her.

"That book should not be in Poppy's hands. She does not know what she's doing."

Penelope laughed in disbelief. "Are you afraid?"

"Don't be absurd."

"Jealous, perhaps?" His sister rolled her eyes. "I saw the way you three nodcocks were whispering by the window. You thought Poppy would use you as her test frog and now you're miffed that she's chosen Captain Gordon instead."

"I am not miffed. I'm worried about her. There's a difference. Besides, he's a useless dolt."

"He's a captain in the Royal Dragoons."

"A commission recently purchased for him by Lord Plimpton.

He's never been to war. He doesn't know what it means to be a soldier. Besides, he's a rogue."

His sister gasped lightly in disbelief. "And you're not?"

"Of course, I'm not. I'm a respected earl. Not to mention I've actually fought in several campaigns against Napoleon, unlike that pizzle Gordon. I'd never take advantage of Poppy. Quite the opposite, I'm duty bound to protect her."

Penelope shook her head and sighed. "Fine, so she isn't to test her feminine wiles on Andrew Gordon."

"Or any other man," he said, casting her a warning glower.

"She has to test them out on someone. Perhaps Angus Carmichael." His sister referred to Wellesford's only doctor who was far too necessary to its citizens to be distracted by this nonsense.

"He isn't suitable."

Penelope frowned. "What's wrong with him?"

Nothing. In truth, Nathaniel liked him. "I thought you wanted her to find someone with a title."

"I do, but Poppy is reluctant. She isn't convinced she would make a proper wife to a nobleman. I think she'd make an excellent countess."

"Stop beating that drum. I am not going to marry your friend."

"Then what about the vicar for Poppy? He's also a good man."

"Adam Carstairs? He isn't suitable either."

"Why not?"

"He's obviously struggling to save his soul." Which was a preposterous statement to make and would not commend him to the Higher Authority. "Besides, she can aim higher."

"Which brings us back to you. Fine, we're agreed then. She'll test *The Book of Love* out on you. I'll let her know that you insisted upon it." Penelope ran off before he had the chance to stop her.

"Bollocks." There were times he wanted to throttle his sister. He watched as Penelope whispered something in Poppy's ear and the girl turned to him in surprise. Her big blue eyes grew wide as saucers and she pursed her lips in obvious displeasure.

Poppy walked toward him, still frowning. "Penelope says you've forbidden me to kiss Captain Gordon."

Dear heaven, who said anything about kissing?

A warm breeze blew across her curls, lightly nudging a few out of place. "Of course, I forbid it." He tucked a wayward strand behind her ear as he spoke to her. It was the natural thing to do. He'd known Poppy forever and there was nothing wrong with treating her as he would his own sister. "You're a guest in my home and therefore under my protection. What would your parents say if I allowed that bounder to kiss you?"

"*I* would be kissing *him*."

"It's the same thing. You are not to lock lips with that man. Your parents would expect me to do all in my power to stop you."

"My parents?" She laughed and shook her head. "I adore them, of course. But I'm not sure they realize I'm here at Sherbourne Manor with you and not at home. There are a lot of Farthingales, and after a while, every head of dark hair and face with blue eyes begins to look the same. I would not be surprised if they counted my sister Violet twice."

"Thinking she was you?"

She cast him a disarming smile.

Poppy always did have a pretty smile, but that did not excuse her idiotic plan to kiss Andrew Gordon. "You are not to go near that man."

"Honestly, Nathaniel. He isn't an ogre. He's quite nice, actually." She had beautiful eyes, too. He'd looked at her often, but why hadn't he noticed this before? Perhaps it was the way the sun glinted on her hair and face just now, seeming to light up her eyes. "I'm sure he wouldn't mind if I kissed him."

"You are to kiss no one." *But me.* Hellfire, that wasn't right. Where did that thought come from?

"Well, that won't work. How am I to test the findings in *The Book of Love* if I can't–"

"Come to me if you have any questions. I'll answer them for you."

"I'm not seeking answers. I'm seeking experience."

"Mother in heaven, are you mad?" He wanted to put his hands on her shoulders and shake her soundly.

"Olivia says that merely reading about the five senses won't do, that to fully appreciate the power of the book, I must perform tests for each sense."

"*Perform* them? On a man?"

"Did you just growl at me? For pity's sake. How else am I to learn about the five senses? You know, the sense of sight, smell, hearing, taste, and touch."

She paused a moment, as though expecting him to respond, and then continued when he merely frowned. "She says the senses of taste and touch are the most dangerous and should not be tested all at once. She recommends I start with the sense of sight first. That seems harmless enough, don't you think?"

He tried to remain calm as they continued to walk along the hedgerows, wondering why he'd allowed himself to be drawn into Poppy's experiments. But to allow this innocent around any other man was a recipe for disaster.

Much of the road was covered in shade cast by tall trees whose branches were lush with green leaves. It made for a pleasant walk even though it was late morning and the sun was shining brightly against the blue sky.

It made for a pleasant walk even though he found this conversation with Poppy most irritating.

He paused when Poppy suddenly stopped and began to turn slowly while in the middle of the road. "What's wrong now?"

"Nothing, Nathaniel. Did you just growl at me again? I was practicing the sense of sight. Looking at my surroundings and doing my best to really take notice." She stopped turning and looked up at him. "Try it, why don't you? Even this road is quite lovely, lined with ancient stone whose crevices are filled with dark green moss. There are tall trees and vibrant green meadows dotted with yellow and purple wildflowers in the distance, and a stream with crystal-clear water runs through the meadows."

He followed her gaze but said nothing.

"Give it a try. What do you see?" She stared at him in expectation.

"This is a silly game. The others are getting too far ahead of us. Let's walk on."

She sighed. "Do you want to know what I see when I look at you?"

An arse? "No."

"A tall, nicely-built man with dark hair and silvery-green eyes... and worries that he's trying to hide from his family."

"I am not worried." He crossed his arms over his chest and frowned at her, but he knew she still saw through his lie. When had she become so perceptive? And how much could she tell simply by looking at him?

"I also see intelligence in your eyes. Strength of purpose. Kindness. Honor." She blushed, no doubt realizing she'd said too much.

He liked her flattering description of him. After all, he prided himself on doing his best for his family and those who worked for him. He cared about his neighbors and the residents of Wellesford. That Poppy realized it and admired him for it was quite satisfying. But she didn't know the rest of it and would be quite scandalized once she did.

"What do you see when you look at me?" she asked.

He was about to say a moppet with unruly dark curls and big blue eyes, but there was a thoughtful intelligence about her that he'd never noticed before.

He eyed her from top to toe, and didn't like the way his heart began to thud within his chest.

"What do you think, Nathaniel?"

Think? He wasn't thinking. He was suddenly caught off guard. Poppy was beautiful.

Stunning, actually.

Why hadn't he realized it before? "The sun's in my eyes. I can't see you clearly. Let's put it off for later."

"Very well." She shrugged her shoulders and resumed walking into town. "It is amazing what one sees when one bothers to look closely. Or rather, what one misses when one isn't really looking carefully. I think that is the strength of *The Book of Love*. It makes you aware of things. It makes you feel sensations you've overlooked for most of your life."

"Right." He'd known the girl for ages and was now taking notice of her for the very first time.

Perhaps there was something to this book.

Poppy placed a hand on his arm, her touch soft and gentle, for the blasted girl did not know how to be any other way. He wanted to find her cloying and dull, but she wasn't. She was just nice. And apparently more perceptive than he'd given her credit for. "You're looking a little tense, Nathaniel. Are you not feeling well?"

"I'm fine."

She shook her head and laughed. "No, you're not. And don't shake your head and insist I'm wrong. We both know I'm not."

"What's your point?"

She turned thoughtful once more. "I'm a quiet person by nature. An observer of the life going on around me. Sometimes, I observe too much. So, I know you are anything but fine. However, I also expect you are not ready to talk about whatever it is that is troubling you."

"I'm not troubled." He didn't know why he felt the need to persist in denying it, especially since Poppy did not believe him.

"I think we would both benefit by *The Book of Love*. I have a proposition for you, Nathaniel."

He groaned inwardly, knowing it could only be more trouble. "What is it?"

"I need to experience more of life. You're the perfect one to help me do it safely. I trust you and know you will always protect me. As for you… well, you need to look at your problems differently in order to find a solution. It is obvious you're stuck and don't know where else to turn. So, why don't we work together toward our mutual goals? *The Book of Love* will help us both."

"Or lead us both to ruin," he said dryly.

"No, it isn't possible. This book is about the power of love to make things right. And where's the harm in that? At worst, it will leave you right where you started. At best, it will fix your problem."

He ran a hand through his hair in consternation. He would move heaven and earth to make his problem go away, but there was no solution to this mess. "No."

She sighed. "Very well, suit yourself. But I shall be reading that book tomorrow morning by the pond. Join me or don't. It is entirely up to you."

"And if I don't?"

"Then I shall kiss Andrew Gordon."

"He's a horse's arse. Blast it, Poppy…" He could do nothing for himself, but he wasn't about to allow Poppy to be ruined by that scoundrel.

Not his Poppy.

Well, she wasn't really *his*.

"Very well, I'll join you. I'll give you four days to work whatever mischief you intend on me. Four days and no more. We're done with those stupid spells in *The Book of Love* once Lady Charlotte arrives. Agreed?"

She nodded reluctantly. "Agreed."

Nathaniel groaned inwardly. Why did he feel as though he'd just struck the worst bargain in his life?

Chapter Two

Nathaniel. Test frog. Day One.
Goal: Low brain connection

Poppy walked to the Sherbourne pond after breakfast the following morning with *The Book of Love* tucked under her arm. She absently nibbled her lip, worried that Nathaniel had changed his mind since he'd been missing from breakfast and was nowhere to be found in the house either.

Her concern was for his sake, not hers. His worries were eating at his insides, although he'd managed to maintain a calm and unperturbed facade whenever in the company of family and friends.

What was he hiding?

She would figure it out in time, for this was her curse, to be able to sense when things were amiss. Observation was her strength. Never actively participating was her weakness. But she had to act now. Penelope Sherbourne was her best friend. She would never allow anything bad to happen to her or her brother. "Nathaniel, you're here. I'm so glad."

He was bent down on one knee, lost in thought while gazing out over the water. He had crouched low so that she did not immediately notice him behind a row of shrubs along the bank of the pond. When he rose and strode toward her, she noticed his casual attire. Buff breeches, a white cotton shirt, brown leather vest, and weathered brown boots. "I said I would join you."

"And you never break a promise."

The flash of pain in his eyes was unmistakable. Ah, he'd broken a promise or was about to do so, and this was the root of his anguish. What had he promised? And to whom?

He avoided her gaze and glanced at his clothes. "The gristmill needed repair. My workers did the hard part. I merely supervised."

She nodded. "Is that how you got those blisters on your hands? By supervising?"

He laughed softly and shook his head. "I may have helped a little."

She smiled at him as she took a seat on the fallen log beside the pond. A majestic oak towered over it and offered plenty of shade to keep them cool under the heat of the summer sun. The grass still carried the scent of dew, although most of it had dried off. "More than a little, I suspect. You seem to enjoy physical labor."

As he drew closer, she noticed that his shirt was damp in spots and sticking to his body. It outlined the contours of his hard muscles and the taper of his trim waist. Beads of perspiration had formed across his brow. Perhaps it was water that he'd splashed across his face and neck to cool himself down. "I'll ride back later to make certain it's properly working."

Poppy nodded.

Whatever this important promise he'd made, it had nothing to do with his estate. Sherbourne Manor was a beautiful home nestled in the Cotswolds, just outside the town of Wellesford. He was the Earl of Welles, and as such, owned the charming town and most of the surrounding land. The farms and mills were thriving, and Wellesford was a bustling hive of activity. "Sit next to me, Nathaniel. We can alternate reading the chapters. I'll start."

He cast her a bored, sacrificial look and reluctantly settled his large frame beside her. Indeed, seated close to her as he was now, she noticed the solid breadth of his chest and the muscled strength of his arms.

"Don't breathe too deeply," he joked. "I'm sweating and still have corn grist in my hair."

"I think I'll survive." Although her heart was suddenly pounding and there was an odd fluttering in her stomach.

She ran her hand lightly over his hair and felt that it was still a little damp. His thick, auburn mane felt soft to the touch. Not at all bristly. It was forward of her to touch him like this, but they'd known each other forever and he did not seem to mind.

And yet, despite having known him for so many years, she suddenly felt the intimacy of the gesture. She suddenly noticed the size and strength of him, and the heat of his body so near to hers. "You've washed most of it off. There's only a speck of grist here or there."

She tried not to make a fool of herself as she moved her hand away and fixed her attention on *The Book of Love*, opening it to the first page and taking a deep breath. But she did not immediately begin to read. "Nathaniel, did you notice how we were using our senses just now? Four of them. The sense of smell." She grinned at him. "And don't cringe. There is nothing wrong with the scent of male exertion, especially when mingled with the sandalwood soap you must have used to wash yourself earlier when you awoke. It's a pleasant, clean smell."

He surprised her by leaning close and inhaling along her neck. "Yours is cinnamon buns."

She laughed. "That isn't me, you dolt. Mrs. Soames made some for breakfast this morning. They were fresh out of the oven and deliciously warm. I couldn't resist, so I brought along two for us to share. That transporting aroma is the buns."

"Then what's your scent?" His lips were achingly close to her skin as he breathed her in again. "Roses. No, lavender. And apples. Sweet. Just ripening. That's you." He arched an eyebrow and grinned. "You're making me hungry."

She handed him one of the buns. "Here. Have both, if you like. I've had my breakfast and won't require more any time soon."

He devoured one and set the other aside, then turned back to her. "You mentioned the sense of smell. Tell me the rest."

"We've covered all five senses now that you've attacked the bun like a ravenous wolf in desperate need of a meal. The aroma of cinnamon aroused your appetite. That's the sense of smell. You ate the bun and obviously enjoyed it. That's the sense of taste. As for the senses of sight and hearing, that's what we are exercising while we sit here, looking at each other as we speak."

He shrugged. "What is so unusual about that? We do it all the time."

She nodded. "But we never think about what we're doing or the significance of the bonds we form whenever we engage each other in conversation. This is what the book is all about."

"You've only spoken of four senses so far. What's the fifth?"

"The sense of touch," she said, struggling to find her voice, for his shoulder had just grazed hers as he'd leaned closer to peer at the pages. Her heart shot into her throat, the unexpected sensation catching her by surprise and sending a thrill through her body. "The touch which happened when I ran my fingers through your hair to brush away the last few flecks of grain. How did you feel when I touched you?"

She hoped he would not turn the question back on her. *Mother in heaven.* Her fingers had tingled the moment she'd felt his damp hair and had yet to stop tingling.

"I don't know. I didn't think about it." He frowned and turned away to gaze at the pond. "It felt natural. It felt comfortable. But I suppose it is to be expected. We've known each other for as long as I can remember. You're like a second sister to me."

He rose and moved away from her.

Was he suddenly uncomfortable around her? Or was she reading too much into the gesture? She hoped it meant that he was having *unbrotherly* thoughts about her, but the answer would be revealed in its own good time.

"Read the first chapter, Poppy. I don't have all day to spend on this nonsense."

He was obviously unsettled, now pacing.

Good.

She hadn't read a word from the book yet. She couldn't wait to see how he'd respond when she began reading to him. She cleared her throat. "Love does not come from the heart but from the brain. It is the brain that sends signals throughout the body, telling you what to feel. Therefore, to stimulate a man's arousal–"

"Hellfire!" Nathaniel returned to her side, his scowl revealing his intention to rip the book from her hands and toss it into the pond. "And Beast actually bought this lewd book for Olivia?"

"It's mine now. Olivia gave it to me." She clasped it protectively to her bosom. "It isn't lewd, it's scientific."

"Since when is arousing a man's… blast it, Poppy! Scientific, my arse. How explicit is this book? What utter nonsense. Hand it over."

"No, I will not. Do stop spouting off like a deranged lizard and let me finish the paragraph. Are you always this intolerant? Do you always jump to the wrong conclusions?"

"I am in complete control of myself. I want that book."

"Are you aware that you growl whenever you are irritated? There, you growled again. Stop it. And I will not give you the book." She kept a tight hold on it. If she could have stuffed it down her bodice, she would have. But the book was too big to fit. In any event, she knew that she was going to win this round, for Nathaniel was not going to grope her to wrestle it away from her.

She stifled a smile, noting his frustration. "Sit down and behave, Nathaniel. If Beast wasn't offended by it, why should you be? Or are you afraid of what it will reveal about you?"

The book remained clutched in her hands, but since she'd already memorized the interesting parts, she began to recite from it, picking up where she'd left off. "Therefore, to stimulate a man's arousal response, one must arouse his sense receptacles in a pleasing way. By touch, taste, sight, smell, and hearing." She glanced up at him. "Do you know what sense receptacles are?"

He sank onto the log beside her, still scowling. "Dare I ask?"

"They are those little parts of our body that make us tingle whenever we are excited about something or someone. But a man's sense receptacles do not operate in quite the same way as those of a female. Nor does a man's brain. It is very different from our own. The author suggests that a man's brain functions on two levels. The low and the high. Or said another way, the simple and complex. When a man's brain is at its lowest functioning level, he is only thinking of sex."

She waited for Nathaniel to explode out of his seat. *Three. Two. One.*

He shot to his feet. "Damn it, Poppy!" His eyes were bulging, the soft, silvery green now mixed with red veins of anger.

She ignored his ranting and pacing and continued to recite, although she wasn't certain he was listening to a single word. "It is his simple brain at work, the one formed thousands and thousands of years ago when creatures first crawled out of the primeval ooze. Very little thought occurs when the man's sexual urges are aroused. Perhaps, no thought at all. But that is the simple brain's purpose. Not to think, but to compel him to breed heirs with any fertile female he comes across."

Nathaniel turned away and sank down onto his haunches as he stared at the water. Tense. Silent. Angry.

Curiously, she thought his anger was directed at himself.

Why would he be angry with himself?

The author suggested that spreading his seed was good.

Nathaniel did not seem to agree, for he had a murderous look in his eyes.

Was that it? Had he spread his seed unwisely and was now agonizing over what to do about it? When had it happened? *Who...* She suddenly knew. *Lady Charlotte Winthrow!* The Duke of Winthrow's daughter. That's why he'd invited them here along with a large party of his elegant London friends.

"Why have you stopped?" He was still turned away and his voice was shaking with anger. "Go on. Let's hear more pearls of wisdom from this ancient tome whose author was too much of a coward to put his name to it."

"Simply because the author remains anonymous doesn't mean the words are less important."

"Fine. Then read on. I'm listening."

She wanted to cry. *Is it possible?* Lady Charlotte was carrying his child and he now had to marry her. There was no question that he would, even though he did not love her. *No, no, no!* She had to be wrong.

"Love," she said, emitting a ragged breath before continuing, "is a higher function of the brain. The important function that makes a man feel the need to protect his family. Wife and offspring. Otherwise, he'd merely spill his seed and then move on, leaving them to be eaten by wolves."

She looked up from the page, unable to hold back her anguish. "Oh, Nathaniel! You needn't hide the truth from me. I know what has happened."

Poppy knows about Aunt Lavinia?

No, it isn't possible. Yet, how could he dismiss her statement as nonsense? The news had the potential to destroy his family. "Nothing has happened," he insisted.

She eyed him skeptically. "I'm not an idiot."

No, she never had been, not even as a little girl.

"What happened isn't anyone's business." And now Poppy of all people claimed to be aware. *Damn it.* How much did she know?

She gazed at him, no sign of indignation or recrimination. Just softness and sadness for his aunt's situation. "You needn't worry that I'll tell anyone," she said gently. "I'd never break a confidence. I give you my promise it will remain a secret between us until you are ready to reveal it. You'll have to tell your family soon. Please, promise me you will before the Winthrows and your other guests arrive."

"How can I?" What he wanted to do was protect Lavinia, this wonderful, dear woman who had always loved him and Penelope. He'd intercepted a blackmail letter to her a few days ago. The secret it contained had shaken him badly. He had no intention of allowing it to destroy his beloved aunt.

His unmarried, maiden aunt.

But this blackmailer claimed she had given birth to a child.

"How can you not?" Poppy asked. "A baby changes everything, doesn't it? It's a little miracle. Your Aunt Lavinia will be–"

"What? Over the moon with joy?" He raked a hand through his hair. "How could you know about this? Did Lavinia confide in you?"

"No. No one had to tell me anything. I'm an observer. Little escapes my notice." She shook her head and sighed. "There is nothing to be done about the past, so let's work on what to do going forward. I think it is important for everyone's happiness."

"Be serious, Poppy. Who can be happy about this? Lord, I don't even know how it happened."

Poppy frowned at him. "You must have some idea."

He sighed. "I do, of course. It was a mistake, obviously. A big, fat one that cannot be taken back. Nor can it be overlooked. How does one approach such a situation?"

Why was he confiding in Poppy of all people? What was it about her that made it easy to release the anguish he'd been trying to bury deep within his soul ever since that letter had come into his possession? But the feeling was clawing its way out, and there was nothing he could do to stop it.

Charlotte and her father would arrive in a couple of days. A dozen more friends would arrive with them. What would they say when Lavinia's scandalous secret came out?

Not that he cared what anyone thought. He only cared about Lavinia and couldn't bear to see her shamed. Of course, the scandal would affect Penelope's marriage prospects. Not that his sister would care either, but he worried for her sake. It wasn't fair that Lavinia's scandal should taint Penelope.

Of course, it wouldn't taint him.

A wealthy earl was forgiven everything.

He wanted to rescind the invitation to Charlotte and her father, and to the others. He wasn't certain why he'd invited any of that fast London crowd in the first place. But Penelope had been so damn quick to pass judgment on Charlotte, he'd come up with the brilliant idea of a country party just to put his wayward sister in her place.

Charlotte at Sherbourne for an entire weekend.

Penelope forced to grin and bear it.

The notion seemed hilarious at the time.

And now this.

The Winthrows would arrive just as the blackmail scheme unfolded.

Under other circumstances, he would not mind seeing Charlotte. She was a beautiful girl, an Incomparable, truth be told. A diamond. A jewel. She'd made no secret of her attraction to him. He'd found her attention flattering.

Perhaps something more would come of it.

He didn't know.

Right now, he was too numb to care.

But Poppy was right. He had to take action immediately if he wanted to save his family.

"Farthingales are renowned for making mistakes. Lots of them," she continued in that soft, lilting voice of hers that he found quite easy to endure. More than merely endure, if he wished to be honest about it, which he didn't.

He had foolishly agreed to be her test frog.

He had not agreed to fall under any magical love spell.

The Book of Love was a hoax and he would prove it to her.

She cast him a smile he refused to find sweet or splendid, and continued her comment. "Indeed, I think the Society gossips can't wait to see what havoc my cousins, Lily and Daffodil, will wreak upon the unsuspecting bachelors when they make their debuts."

He smiled wryly, liking that she was gentle rather than pitying or judgmental.

"But we're also known for loving our children and taking the best care of them. If you need any help, or if you ever have questions about what's involved in carrying a child to term or caring for the child afterward, please ask me. I think I can offer guidance on this subject."

Why would he care about that when Lavinia's secret baby was about as old as he was? Perhaps a few years older. "Poppy, you're an innocent. How can you know these things?"

"Must I keep telling you? I'm an observer." She tipped her chin up as she spoke, but the gesture only made him notice the pink lushness of her lips. "My problem is that I never partake in life. I watch. I assist. Farthingales seem able to knock out children left and right, although some with more difficulty than others. I've attended many births. I've tended to my aunts and cousins when they had to take to their beds because of difficulties during their term. I know a lot about such things. I even assisted Mrs. Fitch in the birth of her youngest boy."

"Why didn't I realize all this about you before?"

She shrugged. "You never asked. You never really looked at me or listened when I spoke."

"Which shows just how much of an arrogant arse I've been." He snorted in disgust. He'd always thought himself so noble and charitable and clever. He'd been a dolt in so many ways. Ignoring Poppy because she was his sister's best friend. Pursuing Charlotte because his smart-mouthed, opinionated sister disliked her.

He didn't like to think he was that petty.

But what if he was?

Charlotte was beautiful, but had he considered courting her for all the wrong reasons? Well, he'd keep his eyes open once she and her father arrived.

What he intended to avoid was a loveless marriage to a woman he did not want. Lavinia had made her mistake and it had cost her dearly.

While he was not about to make the same mistake, this discussion with Poppy had made him consider all that was involved in a marriage. Wife. Children. Protecting them and loving them.

He also worried about Poppy. What if she fell in love with the wrong man because of this ridiculous book of spells? He'd have to keep careful watch over her. He'd feel terrible if amid all these distractions, she wound up with a broken heart.

A sudden thought struck him.

He and Poppy had always had a good rapport. What if it turned into something more on her part and he was the one who inadvertently broke her heart? Poppy trusted him. She admired him. Falling in love with him was a logical next step, wasn't it? Indeed, not so farfetched.

Hell, what if she does fall in love with me?

"Poppy, my sister was not subtle in expressing her wish that you and I might make a love match. That's why she wanted to throw us together with this book. But you know it can never happen, don't you? I can never be more than your test frog."

She nodded. "I know."

"I will still do my best to look after you. I've agreed to give you these next four days, but we can stop now if you've had a change of heart. However, don't consider using Captain Gordon to test the theories in the book. Don't hold out hope that you and he might make a good match. You won't. Be careful around him. There's something about him that puts me on edge. I don't like him. I can't explain why, it's just an uneasy feeling I have whenever I'm in his company."

"How well do you know him?" Poppy couldn't mask her irritation. "You didn't even remember he was at your party. But no matter. I think it's more important that we work on solving your problem first. Unlike Olivia, I'm not desperate to find love. This is only my first Season. I won't turn nineteen until October. I have time, but you don't." She clasped her hands together and gazed up at him. "What will you do? Have you made any plans?"

How does one make plans around a blackmailer? He frowned

lightly. "No."

"None whatsoever?"

"Poppy, don't be naive. This situation must be handled delicately. Utmost discretion. No names mentioned. You said it yourself when reciting the opening paragraph of this book. Men spread their seed. There's no love involved."

"Oh." She cleared her throat. "So, what we have is a man in a bad way one night. Perhaps drunk. A young woman who was there… willing and available."

"It wasn't pretty or magical," he said, staring down at *The Book of Love* and truly worried where it might lead Poppy. Beast had been there to protect Goose from her own misguided attempts to find love.

Unfortunately, it would not be the same for Poppy. Who would protect her if he was not there to do it?

"Nathaniel, I still think we ought to continue these meetings to go over the chapters. This book is about the importance of connections between two people who will be partners for life. It contains great wisdom. I know you don't want to discuss your *secret*, so let's not. But marriage is the most important thing we shall ever undertake. We may not be able to fix all problems, but reading this book will help us to understand how the opposite sex thinks. Perhaps it will help us find true love. Not with each other, of course. So, what do you think? I would like to go on meeting to discuss this book. Would you?"

Since he wasn't going to leave Poppy as easy prey for any rogue, it was easy to answer. "Yes."

"Thank you." She let out the breath she must have been holding. "I hope we both find love. If we open our minds and hearts, I think it will help us to build strong marriages."

He laughed and shook his head.

"Give it a try, Nathaniel. You deserve to be as happy as you possibly can be. But it isn't only about you. It's about the children you and the woman you love will raise."

"Have you always been this irritatingly clever?"

She cast him a gentle smile. "So I've been told by my parents. They seem to think I'm wonderful. But I'm nothing to my cousin, Lily. She's brilliant."

"So are you, it seems." He walked to the edge of the pond and picked up a few stones to skip across the water. "Sherbournes marry for love. I never considered doing otherwise."

"We Farthingales are the same way."

"All the more reason why you must never be forced into a loveless union."

"As I would be with Andrew Gordon?"

He nodded, aware he had to take his own advice and look carefully at Charlotte Winthrow. She wasn't as sweet or understanding as Poppy. But Poppy was too sweet, at times. He didn't like to think the man she chose to marry would destroy her hopes and dreams because she didn't stand up for herself. "At least I can help you. There's a lot I can teach you about men."

He tossed a stone across the water and watched it skip five times before sinking. "Especially when it comes to their lower brain function."

CHAPTER THREE

POPPY STOOD BESIDE Nathaniel by the pond's edge and watched as he tossed stones into the water. They'd only gotten a paragraph into the book, but she could see the taut coil of muscles along his neck and knew any further discussion of its contents would set him off. Not that Nathaniel was the sort to lose his composure, but he was at his wit's end and obviously desperate to find a solution to his problem.

He'd expected to marry for love, for it was the Sherbourne way. He hadn't expected to marry out of necessity to a woman he did not appear to like. Too bad he hadn't realized it before he'd gotten Charlotte Winthrow… in this predicament.

Well, nothing to be done about it now.

She studied his side-arm toss, watching his next stone make six skips before disappearing beneath the water. She picked up one and did the same. But hers merely dropped into the water with a *plop*.

"It's in the wrist, Poppy. Just keep your arm down and flick your wrist."

He came to stand behind her, placing a hand at her waist to draw her lightly up against him. He took her other hand and wrapped it in his while he guided her throw.

Her stone skipped twice.

Her heart skipped multiple times.

He stepped back and cast her an appealing grin. "Better."

She smiled back. "Yes. I'll practice later with Pip. I think this is something he'll have fun doing and it will distract him from terrifying the ducks." Phillip Sherbourne, otherwise known as the devil-child, Pip, was Nathaniel's eight-year-old cousin and his ward. The boy had an active mind that constantly needed to be kept occupied, for he had a diabolical ability to get into mischief.

At the moment, Pip was on a nature walk with Penelope. However, it was too hot to stay out for very long, and she knew he would soon be running to the pond to chase the ducks who were quietly sitting along its grassy edge.

She decided to press on, hoping to read more to Nathaniel before they were interrupted. "Let's get back to the book."

"Must we?" But he nodded. "My brain is ready to burst."

So was hers, but it was important that one of them remain calm.

They settled on the log, and Poppy opened the book again, picking up where she'd left off. She wanted to get through the first chapter today, and they hadn't made it beyond the first page. "Men look for beautiful women. They may define beauty differently, but there is one thing they all agree upon. The woman must appear to be a successful vessel for their sperm or they—"

"Poppy!"

"Oh, don't spout off again, Nathaniel. Do let me finish this passage and you will see the scientific merit in it. If my delicate sensibilities are not offended by the words, then why should yours be? Besides, don't you think I ought to be armed with this information now that I'm in the Marriage Mart and expected to make an enduring love match? Ignorance does not protect me. Knowledge does."

He raked a hand through his hair and sighed. "Lord help me, go on."

"As I was saying, the woman must appear to be a successful vessel for their sperm or they will immediately dismiss her in their minds – too old, too young, too frail, too sickly. So all men will first look for cues that a woman can provide him healthy offspring. At this first inspection, the color of her hair and eyes is not as important as the shape and symmetry of her body."

"Shape and symmetry?"

Poppy nodded. "This is why men look at a woman's… um, chest first when assessing her suitability as a mate. Is that what you noticed about Charlotte?"

"Healthy breasts?" He winced and shook his head. "I have no idea. But if I did, it was only momentary. I'm an unmarried, wealthy earl. Women are always offering their bodies to me. I'm used to it by now."

"Oh, I never realized."

"You wouldn't because you're innocent and would never…" He muttered something under his breath, but he spoke low, and she did not catch what he was saying. Likely, the words were not meant for her delicate ears.

"What else do you like about Charlotte's physical appearance?"

"I don't know." He groaned. "I suppose she has nice hair and pretty eyes. I'll give her that. Is this still my lower brain function at work? The one designed purely for successful mating?"

"Yes, but it is also the first step in making a connection."

He laughed. "I hardly think so."

"You found her pretty. That is a good sign. Many women would make successful mates for you, but very few women will connect with you in the deeper, higher brain manner necessary to make for a happy, committed marriage. You found her body suitable for mating. You also decided she was nice to look at. Now we must find a way to increase the connections and have you fall in love with Charlotte."

"Poppy," he said, frowning at her. "You mustn't speak of Charlotte as though she is my intended bride."

"Oh, I see. No names. Discretion in all things." He was right. And his situation had to be a complete embarrassment. By constantly mentioning Charlotte's name, she might let something inadvertently slip. This was his secret to share, not hers.

He rubbed his hand along the back of his neck. "What would make a father abandon his child and the woman who bore it? Perhaps he was married already? Perhaps he'd died before being able to marry her?"

She took his hand and gave it a light, comforting squeeze. "You'll make a wonderful father." It was possible he would never grow to love his wife, but he'd love their child with all his being.

She felt a sudden ache in her heart. "Oh."

Nathaniel turned to her. "What's wrong?"

"Nothing, the book almost slipped from my hands." What would she have done if he'd approached her while drunk and made amorous overtures to her? She wasn't certain she would have resisted.

It wasn't that he was wealthy or a respected earl. Quite the opposite, it was the warrior, protect-my-woman side of him that would have seduced her. The physical, big-muscled, but kind and gentle… she cleared her throat and concentrated on the task at hand. "Nathaniel, close your eyes and think about what else you like about Charlotte's appearance."

"Why is it so important? She's a pretty girl. The rest of it is… I don't know."

"Well, think about it now."

"Her looks aren't the problem. It's Penelope who's been the thorn in my side. She thinks Charlotte is cold and selfish. She doesn't want me to have anything to do with her. You ought to be reading this book to Penelope, not me."

"We all need to read it. You're no exception. Indeed, isn't it obvious you're the one most in need of taking in its wisdom?" Poppy pursed her lips in thought. "But I'll do what I can to explain it to Penelope. I don't think Charlotte means to be cold to her. The Duke of Winthrow is rumored to be a loud and overbearing man. Charlotte may have had to adapt her behavior to cope with him. He's her father, and she cannot avoid him."

"That's what I've told my sister, but she won't listen." He

shrugged.

"Tell me more about her. Do you find her sweet and warm?"

"Charlotte? Well, no. She isn't like you, Poppy. She isn't nearly as compassionate or caring. Stop talking about her. Let's concentrate on you."

Was he so willing to toss up his hands in surrender and spend the rest of his days in an unhappy marriage? It was common for those of privilege to set up separate households. The husbands would then be free to take on mistresses. The wives would take on lovers once they'd sired the necessary heirs.

But Nathaniel adored his family, and she could not see him living a separate existence from his wife and children.

She did not know Lady Charlotte other than what she'd seen of her at *ton* parties. She was beautiful, indeed. But otherwise, she hadn't been impressed. However, she would not express her feelings to Nathaniel since it wasn't fair to judge a person without really knowing them.

She would try her best to make Charlotte feel welcome when she arrived. They'd never been formally introduced, but this visit would put them in close quarters and give her the chance to know Nathaniel's future wife better.

Nathaniel stretched out on the shaded grass and stared up at the sky. "My mother was a partner to my father in every way. It was more than that. They thrived when in each other's company. Beast and Goose have that. I hope we all experience this happiness when looking at the one we love." He turned to stare at her. "I'm glad you haven't made a cock-up of your life."

"Not yet I haven't. But I'm still young and a Farthingale. Plenty of time to make mistakes." She cast him a wry smile as she sat down beside him.

He brushed back another of her curls that had slipped out of its pin under the force of the light breeze, and smiled back as he tucked it securely behind her ear. "You won't. You're far too clever. Let's work on finding the right man for you."

"You're using me as an excuse to divert your mind from your

problem. Finding someone for me is not an urgent matter. So, let's concentrate on you. I have an assignment for you."

He groaned.

"It isn't so very difficult. Start with making a list for yourself."

"What sort of list?"

"Of the qualities you like about Charlotte."

He sat up and frowned at her. "Charlotte?"

"Yes. Think of the five senses. The look of her. The sound of her laughter. The scent of her body. The touch of her hand."

"You forgot the sense of taste."

She blushed. "It seems too personal to ask about your kissing her. But I suppose it's important and cannot be avoided. How did her mouth feel upon yours? How did she taste to you?" She turned away, suddenly feeling overwhelmed. She'd always liked Nathaniel, but had never spent this amount of time alone with him.

Or noticed the attractive shape of his mouth or the beautiful color of his eyes. They were an extraordinary mix of silvery gray and forest green, and his dark lashes framed them to perfection.

Indeed, she could not deny there was something exciting about having Nathaniel close to her. She breathed in his scent of sandalwood. It was a clean, male scent. And breathed him in again, this time catching the aroma of the cinnamon bun he'd eaten as well as the one that still remained uneaten and wrapped in a plain linen cloth beside him.

The Book of Love was proving to be a revelation and a curse for her.

She had always thought herself a keen observer, but as she began to feel each sensation, to really pay attention to her surroundings and the people around her, she couldn't help but notice this man who had been in front of her all of her life.

Nathaniel.

She liked him.

She liked him very much.

But he was about to have a child with Charlotte.

She wanted to wrap her arms around herself and have a good cry. Nathaniel was lost to her, but would this knowledge stop her from falling in love with him?

She certainly hoped so, but wasn't sure.

NATHANIEL OFTEN MADE lists of the business affairs needed to be attended to, so making the list of Charlotte's strengths and weaknesses Poppy had requested should have been a simple chore. It was late, and everyone had retired to bed hours ago. He was in his chamber, seated at his writing desk with quill pen and parchment in front of him, and a bottle of Scotch whisky beside him. *Uisge beatha*, water of life, it was called. *Source of life.*

He thought it quite ironic since he hadn't felt himself on firm footing ever since returning to England and assuming his role as earl. The war years had changed him, sucked the life and soul out of him, and despite his outward confidence, he could not help but feel his existence was a muck-filled quagmire at the moment.

He'd been feeling this way even before this matter with Lavinia had come up.

He drained the glass he'd poured for himself, savoring the warmth of the amber liquid as it slid down his throat. "Charlotte," he muttered, attempting to concentrate. He wanted to be diligent in this exercise, but he wasn't certain how it would help him find the blackmailer.

However, Poppy wanted him to do this, and he did not wish to disappoint her.

He returned to the task of drawing up his list.

The look of Poppy.

He scratched it out and tried again. The look of Charlotte. *Eyes, beady and assessing. Smile, insincere.*

He scratched that out and gave up for the evening.

He wasn't being fair to Charlotte.

He'd try again tomorrow, perhaps think more clearly after a

good night's rest.

He undressed and set his clothes aside for his valet to attend to in the morning. His skin felt damp from the August heat. He'd left his window open and crossed to it to soak in the breeze, for he needed to cool down. But the air was laden with moisture and the wind was gusting, a sign that rain was in the offing.

Even the moon looked odd tonight, a big, red ball hovering low over the pond. A blood moon that the villagers believed was a harbinger of ill tidings to come. Ill tidings, indeed. A few more days and the Winthrows would arrive.

Would Lavinia's blackmailer use their visit to ruin his aunt?

He peered into the darkness. His quarters faced the front of the house. His view was of the drive leading up to the manor and its elegant gate. From his window, he also saw the pond and the meadow separating his manor house from Gosling Hall where Beast and Olivia now resided.

He shook his head and quietly laughed. Whoever would have thought the mighty and powerful Alexander Beastling, Duke of Hartford, would fall for his Little Goose? That's what Olivia had been to Beast. He'd given her the pet name because she was a little girl and her name was Gosling.

Nathaniel wanted what the newlywed pair had, but how was he to find love while his soul was still in pain? He'd recognized the same pain in Beast and Thad, and imagined most men who'd fought in wars, didn't matter which ones, would not easily forget those years out of their lives.

Some overcame it and moved on.

He hadn't yet.

Bah.

He shook off the grim thoughts that seemed to plague him in the dark of night. Lavinia was the urgent problem. He wasn't ready to reveal the blackmail plot to his family or friends, but knew Beast and Thad would listen and offer their support when the time came.

He hoped it would never come. But how did one go about

finding a blackmailer whose identity was unknown? He'd been quietly asking around, discreetly questioning his staff and others in town about anything odd they'd noticed recently.

Nothing had turned up.

It also bothered him that Poppy had guessed Lavinia's situation. How could she know? Had he inadvertently revealed something? Had Lavinia confided in her about the child she'd given up? He wouldn't be surprised, for Poppy had a trustworthy manner about her and was never one to pass judgment. She was the sort of person one turned to when needing to unburden one's soul.

What will Charlotte and her father make of her?

He did not like that Charlotte's guest bedchamber would be next to Poppy's. In truth, he did not like that Poppy would be here when the Winthrows and the rest of his upper crust friends arrived.

He could make up a pretext to send Poppy away.

No, that wouldn't work. Neither Penelope nor Lavinia would ever allow her to go. They adored Poppy. She would have to stay, just as she had most summers throughout her life, in the guest bedchamber she'd always been given, the one next door to Penelope's bedchamber. The one that overlooked the garden so Poppy could enjoy the flowers in full bloom and the lush, green trees.

Now that Beast and Olivia were settled at Gosling Hall, he was going to give Olivia's room to Charlotte, and her father would take Beast's quarters. He wasn't eager to have the Duke of Winthrow or his daughter in his home just now, but he would have to make the best of it.

After all, he'd invited them.

He hoped Penelope and Thad would behave themselves, but those two were hotheaded and more likely to stir things up rather than calm them down.

No, Poppy was the voice of reason. She was the friend who would stand by Lavinia and love her with all the strength in her compassionate heart once the scandal broke.

He hoped Charlotte and her father would not eat the sweet girl alive.

He turned away and fell naked into his bed.

Moonlight filtered in through his window, its glow an ominous, dark red instead of its usual shimmering silver.

Still, he imagined Poppy beside him, moonlight falling across her peaceful face.

"Gad, you're an arse." He was only thinking of Poppy because she was a comforting presence and he was used to having her in his home.

That he now wanted her in his bed was proof of how twisted his mind was at the moment. Such thoughts would only lead him into deeper trouble. She was his sister's best friend. She was the gangly, scrawny girl who spent summer weekends at their home. "Keep thinking of her as that."

Because she did not deserve to be thought of as the luscious young woman he ached to hold in his arms. Acting upon such thoughts would bring her down along with him, and he'd never do anything to hurt Poppy.

So why couldn't he shake the feeling he was about to hurt her deeply?

Chapter Four

Nathaniel. Test frog. Day two.
All hope lost.

IT CAME AS no surprise to Nathaniel that he was out of sorts and had hardly closed his eyes by morning. It was early yet, but he knew his staff had already begun their day. He and Thad had promised to take Pip riding with them. He'd bought the boy a gentle mare that would be easy enough to control, provided Pip did not do anything foolish.

Hah! That was a lark. Pip had an uncanny ability to do precisely the thing you did not want him to do. Obviously, a trait that ran in the Sherbourne family. If Pip behaved, it was because of his desire to ride with the men and he knew the privilege would be revoked if he played any of his tricks.

But it was raining hard and there would be no riding this morning.

He washed and dressed and strode into the dining room in time for breakfast. Thad, Penelope, and Poppy were seated at the table. Pip had been and gone by the look of the trail of crumbs and the soiled linen beside an empty plate. "Devil-child has eaten, I see."

His sister laughed. "I don't know why we allow him to take his meals with us. He can't sit still for more than five minutes, if that. He dropped a spider in Poppy's eggs this morning."

Nathaniel turned to her with concern. "Poppy, I'm sorry."

She smiled at him, obviously not at all distressed by Pip's antics. "I ought to be flattered. I believe this is his way of telling me that he likes me."

Thad turned to Penelope with a smirk. "What do ye think, Loopy? Shall I place a spider in your eggs as a peace token between us?"

Nathaniel's sister arched an eyebrow. "Wouldn't you love to do just that? A big, hairy poisonous one, I'll wager."

Thad sighed. "Right, one that will sting you in your uptight arse and–"

"Children, behave." Nathaniel frowned at both of them. At times, they were worse than Pip, who was merely a child and didn't know any better. "Where's Aunt Lavinia?"

Poppy responded, giving him a meaningful glance. "She wasn't feeling well this morning. Nothing too serious, just some aches and pains in her bones. They'll pass along with this rainstorm, I'm sure."

"I'll look in on her a little later," his sister said. "She might enjoy the company."

Thad set down his coffee cup. "I'll keep Pip occupied, perhaps teach him how to play chess. We'll see how long it takes before the lad tips over the board."

Nathaniel thanked his friend. "I have some documents to review this morning. It shouldn't take me long."

Poppy cleared her throat.

He turned to her. *Right, the damn list.* "Give me an hour and then come into my study with that book." He scowled at Thad and Penelope when they began to chortle. "There is no magic within its pages. I'm only indulging this nonsense to make certain you fools don't lead Poppy astray."

He finished his breakfast and retired to his study to take care of Wellesford matters that needed his immediate attention. New contracts for the gristmill. Repairs needed to some of the tenant farms. Donation toward a new roof on the vicarage house. Why were these church roofs always in need of repair?

He looked up when he heard a light knock at his door. "Enter."

Poppy walked in with *The Book of Love* in hand, but took no more than a couple of steps forward before stopping. "It's been an hour, Nathaniel. Are you ready for me or shall I come back later?"

He sighed as he tucked away his papers. "I'm ready. Come in and shut the door."

She hesitated.

He rose to do it himself. "No one in my household will remark on it. My servants are discreet, and neither Thad nor my sister will notice or care since they're always too busy trying to murder each other."

She laughed and took the offered seat across the desk from him. He settled back in his chair. "I haven't made the list. I tried last night. Couldn't get my mind around it."

"We can work on it together now." She placed the book on his desk. It did not look particularly extraordinary, just old with its red-leather binding now faded. There was no gold leaf or ornate artwork amid the lettering as one would find in an illuminated manuscript. "Take out a sheaf of writing paper and we'll start. Let's work on the sense of sight first. What are Charlotte's best features? That ought to be easy enough. She's a pretty girl."

Why was she pushing Charlotte on him again? Just because he'd invited her this weekend? "Why don't we start with making a list of your attributes, Poppy?"

Poppy sighed. "No, it's best if we use Charlotte for this exercise."

"Very well, but you are not to use Andrew Gordon for your part. Got that?"

She rolled her eyes. "Yes, you've made it quite clear. Back to your assignment."

"Right, her best features. She has nice hair. A pretty gold color. Her eyes are blue, I think." He shrugged. "I suppose they are. They're nice enough. Not a lot of intelligence behind them. A little dull, in truth."

"Keep to the point, Nathaniel. Think of her strengths."

"She has a nice body. Her outward looks aren't the problem."

"That's good. So, if you look at her as though meeting her for the first time, you'd find her very pretty."

He nodded.

"A suitable vessel into which to spill my seed," he said ruefully. Had Olivia put Beast through this nonsense? He supposed if his friend could tolerate it, then he could as well.

"Let's move on to the sense of hearing. Do you like the sound of her voice? Her laughter?" Poppy leaned forward as he began to write. "You're frowning again. Why is this so difficult for you?"

"It's a stupid assignment."

"Goodness, were you always this bad-tempered as a schoolboy? Do stop frowning. Does she have a nice voice? A nice laugh?"

"I never paid attention. I don't think she laughs much."

"That's interesting." Poppy was staring at him as though expecting him to drop a brilliant revelation. "Nathaniel, why do you think she never laughs?"

He shrugged again. "I didn't say she never laughs, only that I hadn't noticed. Perhaps she doesn't find me funny. Perhaps I wasn't listening to her when I ought to have been."

"Perhaps she's sad."

Poppy had the softest way of kicking his arse to Bedfordshire and back, showing him to be the callous dolt he was. But this was the strength of women, especially Poppy, to get into another person's heart and sense what they were feeling.

The possibility that Charlotte was sad had never entered his mind. "You put me to shame, Poppy. I never once considered… why do you think she's unhappy?"

"Don't you know? You'll have to talk to her and put her mind at ease."

He arched an eyebrow and cast her a wry, mirthless smile. "We all know how productive that will be. Men don't listen very well, do they?"

"We listen for different things. Men tend to be direct. If I were to tell you that I hurt, you would ask, 'Where does it hurt?' I'll fetch a doctor, and that would be the end of the conversation. But women listen for the feelings behind the statement. Why does it hurt? How does it hurt? Who caused your hurt?"

She glanced at *The Book of Love*, as though attempting to absorb its wisdom. Nathaniel did not believe her cleverness came from those chapters. Poppy had a natural intelligence and a genuine compassion.

"Let's move on, Poppy. But would you mind if I took this book for a few hours? I'd like to read it. I promise not to damage it in any way. I still want to go over the list of senses with you first. This will be a means of reinforcing what you've taught me."

He ran a hand through his hair, wanting to say more to her but not certain how to proceed. Perhaps saying nothing was best for now. Poppy was showing a side of herself that he'd never known existed. Of course, he hadn't been looking. Or listening. "We've covered sight and hearing. What next?"

"The sense of smell. What is her scent? Did it attract you to her?"

He sighed. "I don't know. I think I was drunk when we first met."

"You were?" She shook her head in confusion. "Well, you weren't always drunk. Just that one time, right? Oh, dear. You have such a blank look on your face." She pursed her lips in thought. "Seriously, Nathaniel. Why is this so difficult for you?"

Feelings, damn it.

"I have a lot on my mind. Why don't we start with something simpler? You're right in front of me. Why don't we try this exercise with you?"

"Very well. What's my scent this morning?"

"Cinnamon."

She laughed. "You really do enjoy your cinnamon buns, don't you? I think you are still hungry."

He grinned. "Always. But you also… I think of roses and lavender and country gardens when I'm around you. Pink roses for your cheeks and lips. Blue lavender for your eyes. There's something clean and refreshing about your scent. An apple orchard when the trees are first blossoming. Or wild strawberries, perhaps. Warm, fragrant. Lazy summer days."

"That's quite good, actually. Well done, Nathaniel. Now think of Charlotte."

He groaned. "Hellfire, I don't know."

"Yes, you do. You're resisting your feelings. Think of the first time you met her. Where were you?"

"Crowded ballroom. Around April or May. Maybe May. The weather was warm. Maybe it was a particularly warm day in April. All that comes to mind is overly perfumed, sweating bodies."

"But not Charlotte's, or you wouldn't have gone near her."

"I suppose not. Poppy, I don't remember. But I'll make sure to take note of her scent when she arrives. Not immediately, of course. She'll smell of dirt and sweaty horses."

Poppy emitted a laughing groan. "You sound like a petulant little boy. Even Pip would roll his eyes at you. Yes, do wait until she washes the scent of travel off her."

"So where does that leave us? Touch and taste?" Lord, he was not going to go into detail about the dream he'd had last night. Poppy in his bed. The taste of her hot skin and the after scent of sex, utterly unsuitable for Poppy's ears, and not something he was proud of.

Poppy's cheeks were flaming, as though she knew what he was thinking. But she couldn't possibly. "Oh, dear," she said with a light shake of her head. "You look as though you'd rather walk across a bed of nails than talk further on the topic."

"Quite so."

"Nathaniel, it seems to me that you aren't particularly attracted to Charlotte. If that is so, then what made you…"

"Invite her this weekend?"

She nodded. "Yes, if you wish to put it that way."

How else was he to put it? He'd invited Charlotte. She'd accepted. He now regretted it. "It's complicated."

"That's what men say when they are required to discuss their feelings."

"We are not going to discuss my feelings." He raked a hand through his hair and emitted a low growl. The blasted girl was going to push him too far. Protecting Lavinia was the urgent problem. Finding himself a wife was of secondary importance. He was a wealthy earl. A much sought-after bachelor. He had only to crook his finger and a dozen debutantes would come running.

He didn't even have to offer marriage.

They'd willingly come to his bed.

"No talk of feelings," he repeated when Poppy cast him a soft, heart-melting look that made him want to wrap her in his arms and hungrily explore her silken body while he forgot about the demons that still gripped him.

He had yet to shed the darkness of war, yet to forget the pain and sorrow and loss.

She stared at him.

"Damn it, Poppy." He was not going to discuss the war with her, but her gaze pierced his soul, and he knew she'd listen to his innermost fears, his anger and frustrations. She'd listen and be gentle. He could open his heart to this girl, expose its raw and painful wounds, and she would treat them with exquisite tenderness and compassion.

But the two of them were in his study to speak of love, not to dissect the horrors he'd experienced in wartime.

She glanced out the window. "I do wish it would stop raining. You look like the walls are about to close in around you. In truth, you look like you want to topple the walls down around my head."

"Like Sampson toppling the walls of the temple and crushing all within it?" He rose and came around the desk to stand beside her. "No, any irritation or anger I feel is aimed at me."

Poppy's lips were pursed and her brow furrowed in thought. He studied her and said nothing, now eager to know what she was thinking.

"Why are you so angry with yourself, Nathaniel?"

"Isn't it obvious?" He shrugged. "I like to be in control. But events seem to have taken control of me."

"Of course. And you don't like the feeling of helplessness."

"Feelings again," he muttered. "I handle my problems. I don't like when they have me by the throat."

"My parents taught me that problems are a series of events when taken apart are harmless, but when put together in a particular way cause chaos. First, stop blaming yourself for what has happened. And don't blame anyone else either."

He snorted. "No blame?"

"That's right. If you take away the blame, what do you have left?"

"Hell, I don't know. You seem to be the one with all the answers."

She rolled her eyes and laughed softly. "I certainly do not have any answers. I've experienced nothing. I'm the sheltered, ignorant one."

He drew closer, unable to help himself. "You're not ignorant."

"I most certainly am about men and their desires." She cleared her throat and gave a little 'eep' when he took another step closer. "Think of your problems as steps on a staircase or rungs on a ladder. The first step might be something unimportant and seemingly unrelated. A broken gristmill wheel, for example. And then you find out it can't be repaired for a month. So, you stop by your club—assume you are in London—for a drink because you are angry and frustrated."

He moved away from her and walked to the hearth, staring into the empty grate. It was summer, and no fire would be lit unless the weather turned exceptionally cold. "Poppy, stop. These feelings you're trying to evoke from me have nothing to do with love."

She came to stand by his side. "What are they about?"

"The opposite of love."

"War?"

He arched an eyebrow in surprise. "The opposite of love is hate. What made you say war?" Which is what he had been thinking, and she'd gotten it right. But how had she known? "Never mind. Let's put an end to this conversation before it turns ugly."

"Nathaniel, you're shaking." She began to stroke his arm as though to comfort him. Did the girl realize she had put his heart in an iron clamp and was painfully twisting it? He didn't want to answer her. "I'm not afraid of ugly conversations."

Oh, but she would be if he spoke of the dreadful day his regiment returned to London and the sight of all those coffins laid out in a row on the docks.

"Nathaniel, let's keep no secrets. We've known each other all of our lives. If we can't trust each other, then who can we trust?"

Everything about Poppy was soft and soothing.

He closed his eyes a moment to allow her warmth and sweetness to soak deeply under his skin. "It isn't a question of trust, Poppy. You know I trust you. Even after you stole my clothes and left me naked in the pond."

"I can assure you, I've reformed." She cast him an impish smirk, no doubt realizing this conversation had been headed in a dark direction and both of them were now eager to lighten it. "Do you wish to speak of those happier times?"

Despite himself, he laughed. "You are manipulating me."

"I most certainly am not. It isn't in my nature, as you well know. So, what shall it be? You don't wish to speak of difficult times, do you?"

"No." He'd formed bonds with the men in his regiment that were stronger than any he'd ever make again. Thad and Beast understood because they'd also gone off to fight. The three of them had always been friends, but the war had brought them even closer. He'd wept for joy the night he realized they'd all survived.

But memories of war still brought him pain.

And memories of their last summer at Sherbourne before they all went off to war still brought him exquisite peace and contentment. "You girls were about ten-years-old at the time," he said, his voice sounding raw and raspy even to his ears. "You and Penelope and Olivia. We'd just spent a summer here, you with your friends and me with mine."

"Thad and Beast. I remember it well. It was an idyllic summer, wasn't it?"

He laughed. "Until the day you caught us swimming naked in the pond and stole our clothes. You knew we couldn't chase after you."

Poppy's smirk turned into a broad, unrepentant grin. "I'd never done anything so wicked in all my life. Penelope was the one with the streak of mischief. She goaded me and Olivia. She grabbed Thad's clothes. I went along and ran off with yours, but Olivia didn't have the heart to take Beast's. I couldn't believe it. She neatly folded his clothes and left them by the pond for him to find."

"You could have done the same with mine."

She shook her head. "Yes, but I was taken up in the moment and rather enjoying my wicked self. I knew I'd have to deal with the consequences later, but in that moment, I felt giddy and powerful… and deliciously naughty."

"It was one of those silly, utterly carefree days. It was a day of laughter and innocence. Shortly afterward, Beast, Thad, and I went off to war. Those were years of hardship, chaos, and madness. There was so much death and destruction."

She still had her hand on his arm. "I'm so sorry."

He liked the touch of her hand. There was magic in the girl, not the book. He wasn't going to tell her so. He didn't want to talk about the sense of touch. In truth, he didn't want to talk about the war, either. But Poppy made it easier to get these difficult thoughts out.

In less than a day, the girl had managed to have him talking about problems he'd buried deep inside of him and sworn never to let escape. He'd handled the rage and frustration of war, the senseless killing. What he hadn't been able to overcome was the unfairness of it all.

Would he be able to talk things through like this with Charlotte? Would Charlotte's touch feel anywhere near as wonderful as the gentle touch of Poppy?

Poppy still had her lips pursed in thought.

Those pouty, beautiful lips that he must have been dead as a donkey not to notice before yesterday.

Her silence got him talking again. It was that or give in to the desire to kiss her.

He wasn't going to kiss Poppy.

No, indeed. He refused to consider it. "The battles were difficult, to be sure. But what I found hardest was being called back home when my father passed away. I assumed his title, Earl of Welles, and was handed all this bounty." He waved his hand to encompass the house and its grounds as well as the entire village of Wellesford. "But my regiment was still on the Continent fighting Napoleon. I wanted to be with them. I belonged there, not here."

His voice hitched as he spoke the last. "We all thought the war was over when Napoleon was first exiled. But he escaped and built up his army again. My regiment was still in France. They were decimated in a brutal battle shortly before Waterloo."

Poppy inhaled lightly.

"All those years of hard fighting and hardly a man lost. Then suddenly, just three months before the end of the war..." Tears clouded his eyes. He would have been ashamed to show his weakness in front of anyone else. But Poppy was different. She had stripped his feelings raw and did not make him feel the lesser for it.

She put her arms around him. "What a terrible blow. I'm so

sorry, Nathaniel. Your grief must be beyond imagination."

"You spoke of rungs on a ladder. Idyllic summer. That's one. Going off to war. That's two. Coming home. That's three. Learning the fate of my regiment. That's four. What's next? Scandal and ruin?" He sighed raggedly. "How many more rungs are there? Does it matter? The night of the battle that destroyed my regiment, I was attending a London ball, having a merry time being chased by beautiful women who offered me their bodies at every turn. They cared not a fig about me. They wanted my wealth and title. I should have…"

"Gone back and died along with your men? Oh, Nathaniel, you know that is not true. You'll do far more good in the world by living. You're in a position to help the survivors. Perhaps you can do something for the families of those who did not survive."

He nodded. "I've told myself that. I've taken steps, but the problem is so big, anything I do seems small and inconsequential."

"It isn't. Even if one life is made better. One family helped. But I know the sort of man you are. You've probably helped dozens by now."

"When I heard the news, I was frustrated and angry, ashamed of myself for not being there when they needed me. The bodies were shipped home in early May. I went to the docks to lend assistance, looking forward to greeting the survivors as they walked down the gangplank. I was not prepared for the number of coffins stacked under the heat of the morning sun. There were so many, Poppy. I couldn't bear it."

He turned away and took a moment to regain what little composure he had left. "So how can we speak of love and the spells in that silly book? How can I think of you or Charlotte or any young woman when my heart is still filled with rage at the unfairness of it all?"

He grunted in disgust. "Do you want to know the cruelest jest of all?"

Poppy's hand still rested on his arm as though it was frozen and she was afraid to move it.

"My heart is so badly damaged, Poppy. Yet, I still want this book of spells to work. So we're going to read through every one of those stupid chapters. And even though I'm unlikely ever to find love, I know you will. I'll make it my mission to find you the one man who will make you so damn happy, you'll have stars in your eyes and buttercups sprouting from your lips whenever you speak of him."

He returned her stare, losing himself in the enchanting blue of her eyes. "There you have it. Now you know more about me than anyone else alive."

Now that he'd poured his heart out to her, he wanted to kiss her.

Lord. Had he gone utterly insane?

Kiss Poppy?

He'd already done worse in his dreams.

She said nothing for the longest while. "Nathaniel..." Her voice was soft and sweet and aching. She reached up and kissed him on the cheek. It was nothing like the kiss he wished to give her, not hot or raw or possessive. Yet, the soft press of her lips stirred something deep within him. A hope. *Yes.* That's what Poppy was, hope and brightness. "Thank you for sharing this with me. I'll never betray your confidence."

"I know."

She nodded and walked out, quietly shutting the door behind her.

She'd left *The Book of Love* with him.

He intended to read it cover to cover. Perhaps it would hold the answer to the question now burning in his mind.

Why did he yearn to kiss Poppy?

No, that wasn't quite right.

Why did he yearn to kiss no one but Poppy?

CHAPTER FIVE

POPPY WAS QUITE shaken when she walked out of Nathaniel's study. She wanted to write to her parents, asking them for guidance, but knew she couldn't. She'd promised Nathaniel. And what could her parents tell her other than to be a friend to him and honor his secret?

She'd read *The Book of Love* several times over now and understood that love came when two people formed bonds with each other. The first chapters spoke of the male brain and its structure. The lower brain, the sexual one, that only thought of mating with a female perceived as fertile. The later chapters spoke of the higher brain, the one that dealt with love. The one that told his heart, this is the one for you.

A woman's brain only had the higher brain function, for her purpose was to protect her offspring. As the book stated, protect her young so that they would not be eaten by wolves. So, the woman's brain looked for the one who would protect her and her children.

Poppy's brain was not simply sending a message to her heart, it was pounding it out, *Nathaniel is the one for you.*

How could her heart tell her this?

Nathaniel was going to marry Charlotte.

She glanced in the parlor and noticed Penelope, Thad, and Pip in a corner by the window, hovered over a chessboard. Lavinia, she was pleased to see, had come downstairs and was also in the parlor, seated at her small writing table penning a letter to a friend. Perhaps to Beast's aunt, Duchess Matilda, who had returned to London for a fortnight in order to give her nephew and his new bride time alone.

Lavinia's black and tan spaniel, Periwinkle, was curled on her lap, his usual place of honor. His ears perked and he lifted his head when he noticed her by the door.

Poppy was too overset at the moment to join them.

Lavinia was Nathaniel's elderly aunt. Pip was his impish ward. Penelope was his smart-mouthed sister. Nathaniel took care of them all, not merely providing a roof over their heads or food and generous pocket money, but keeping them all together as a family.

He could have set them up in a separate residence, sent money as needed, and spent his days enjoying his bachelor life. But this was not Nathaniel's way. He was a protector to the depths of his soul, not only of his family but also of his friends.

She turned on her heels and strode back to his study, barging in without knocking. He was casually seated in his chair behind his desk, reading *The Book of Love*. He looked up with a frown that quickly turned into a wry smile when he realized she had been the one to walk in unannounced. "Poppy?"

"When Goose's parents died and her guardian took her away from Gosling Hall, letting it fall into ruin, were you the one who looked after it?"

"It meant a lot to Goose. I couldn't let her home–"

"Why didn't you tell us?" She emitted a ragged breath. "You did it quietly and never took the credit for it."

He set aside the book and rose as she approached him. "I helped out a friend, that's all. I didn't do it for the accolades. I did it for Goose."

"Nathaniel…"

He arched an eyebrow. "Yes, Poppy?"

She stood so close to him that she could see the silvery flecks in his eyes and count them. She wanted to reach up and kiss him soundly on his nicely-shaped lips. She wanted to throw herself into his arms. "Thank you."

She turned to walk away, but he took her hand to hold her back. *Heavens, his touch!* His hand was big and warm and felt so perfect as it circled around hers. "What I did for Goose is nothing to what you are doing for me. I sent over a groundskeeper and a few maids on occasion, something anyone could have done. A little money tossed here or there was something I could easily afford. But what you are doing for me, that's priceless."

She thought he might kiss her. Their lips were close enough that she felt his breath on hers.

She wanted him to kiss her.

"I'd given up hope on a love marriage. But you've helped me see things from another perspective. If I find happiness in my marriage, it will be because of you."

Her heart crashed to the floor. "Yes, well… that's what friends do for each other. Quietly and without accolades."

She slipped her hand out of his and summoned all the pride she could muster while walking out of his study. She shut the door behind her and fell against it with a silent sob.

Then raced upstairs to her bedchamber to fall onto her bed in tears.

WHEN THE RAIN stopped at midday, Beast and Olivia came over from Gosling Hall in time to join them for luncheon. "Where's Nathaniel?" Beast asked, noticing his absence. "Is he hiding from you, Poppy?"

She cast him a smile. "No, quite the opposite. He's taken *The Book of Love* quite seriously. I think he's still locked away in his study reading it."

Penelope's eyes rounded in surprise and she shot to her feet. "You trusted my brother with the book? He'll destroy it."

Poppy rolled her eyes. "No, he won't. He's embraced the wisdom."

Thad cast her a dubious look. "Embraced it? I have to get my hands on that book."

"When pigs fly," Penelope snapped back. "I'm getting that book next, and you will never get your big Scottish paws on it."

Poppy turned to the sound of rumbling laughter behind her. Nathaniel was standing in the doorway. He cast her a private smile before turning to his sister. "I shudder to think of that book in your hands," he teased, but there was an undercurrent of warning in his words. "You must promise me you'll never use it to hurt Thad."

Penelope appeared ruffled. "I'd never hurt him. How could you think I would?" She turned to stare at Thad. "Even if I did use you as a test frog–"

"Bollocks." Thad ran a hand through his dark red hair. "Don't even think about it."

"I'm not. That book is too powerful, and I am not going to risk your falling in love with me." She raised her hand when he began to protest. "Don't worry. I'll be testing it out on someone who actually has a chance of liking me. I know that won't be you."

"Good, because I have no intention of sitting quietly and allowing you to dissect me. I'm not a damn frog."

"Right, you're not a frog. You're a big, Scottish–"

"Stop! The two of you." Poppy wanted to say something more to the pair, but couldn't find the words. How could she spout an opinion when she was using *The Book of Love* to bring Nathaniel and Charlotte together? She hadn't used a single test on Nathaniel. If anything, she was purposely giving him all the answers. She had no intention of ever testing him. How could she risk his falling in love with her?

Not that she believed for a moment it might happen, for he was too caught up in his problems to look beyond his own nose.

But in helping him, she'd put her heart at risk and it was now breaking. She never realized falling in love could hurt so badly. "Excuse me," she mumbled and ran out of the room.

She hurried upstairs and grabbed a shawl, then attempted to slip out the back stairs. The sun was now peeking out from what had moments ago been a solid wall of gray. But the gray clouds were now breaking up to reveal patches of blue sky. The ground was still muddy, but she had on her sturdy walking boots. They could withstand getting sucked into those small, muddy pools that had formed in the roadway.

She cut across the back garden, intending to take the shortcut to Wellesford and uncertain what she would do once there. Perhaps she'd visit Miss Billings, the local bookshop owner, and share a cup of tea with her after browsing through her shop. Getting away from Sherbourne Manor and its handsome owner seemed of great importance at the moment.

"Oh, bother." She frowned as she glanced down, noticing she'd dirtied her gown when shoving open the gate that stood along the stone fence running the perimeter of the Sherbourne property. Everything was still soaked from the recent rain, and now mud and wet leaves had stuck to the delicate lavender muslin.

She managed to brush most of it off, but streaks of dirt still lingered along the hem and across the bodice. Nathaniel's capable staff would clean it, hopefully without too much fuss.

"Miss Farthingale," she heard someone call from behind her.

The voice was masculine. Deep and rumbling, but cheerful. She turned toward the sound with a smile. "Good afternoon, Dr. Carmichael."

He caught up to her within a few strides. "You shouldn't be walking on your own. Where are your friends?"

"Just sitting down to lunch, but I wasn't hungry." It wasn't quite true, but she did not wish to discuss the real reason. "I have an errand to complete in town, so I thought I'd take care of it now that the sun has come out."

He glanced up at the sky, then returned his gaze to her. The doctor's eyes were a rich, nut brown and his hair was a dark, reddish-brown, a little darker than Thad's. Angus was his given name and he'd come down from Scotland years ago to set up his practice here in Wellesford. He was a little older than Nathaniel and his friends, but not by more than a couple of years. "I'm headed that way now. I'll escort you."

She would have preferred to be alone with her thoughts, but knew it would not happen. Dr. Carmichael had those same protective instincts as Nathaniel, Beast, and Thad. He would never allow her to continue on her own, it mattered not that the town could be seen in the distance.

"Were you looking in on Mrs. Fitch and her children?" she asked as he fell into step beside her.

He nodded. "The little one, Walter, fell and sprained his wrist. Nothing too terrible. The lad was off and playing with his brothers and sisters as soon as I'd finished binding it."

"Oh, I'm so glad." She had helped deliver Walter into the world and it was not something she would ever forget.

She'd only been fourteen at the time. She, Penelope, and Goose had been walking into town one beautiful summer's day when they'd encountered Mrs. Fitch struggling by the side of the road. She was in labor. Her three small children were crying beside her, all of them too young to run into town on their own for help. Penelope had taken on that task while Goose had taken the children aside and distracted them with stories. It had been left to her to assist Mrs. Fitch with the birth.

So, she did.

And the babe came out just as Penelope returned with Dr. Carmichael. She'd gone to him since the midwife was nowhere to be found. He'd allowed Poppy to remain by his side, explaining each step as he worked to clean up the afterbirth and snip the umbilical cord.

"Do you remember Walter?"

She nodded and gave a merry laugh. "How could I forget him? The moment he entered the world is seared into my memory. I was afraid Mrs. Fitch was going to name him Poppy. Thankfully, she came to her senses in time."

He grinned at her. "What? Don't you know? She and her husband named the lad Walter Poppy Fitch. Did no one ever tell you?"

Her eyes widened in surprise. "No. Are you jesting? You know I'm awfully gullible."

"Upon my oath, it is the truth. You can ask Vicar Carstairs if you don't believe me. Walter P. Fitch is the lad's name, and that P stands for Poppy."

She shook her head and sighed. "That boy will hate me forever."

He gave a light groan. "Miss Farthingale, no man will ever hate you. I'm surprised you haven't at least a dozen beaus following you wherever you go."

"I fear I must disappoint you. I haven't a single one."

He arched an eyebrow and glanced back. "Seems you do have one. An earl, no less."

"What?" She turned to follow his gaze. Nathaniel was striding toward them.

"Good afternoon, Dr. Carmichael." But he was looking at her and frowning. She supposed he wasn't happy that she had simply run off.

"A beautiful afternoon it is, Lord Welles. I was just commenting on it to Miss Farthingale."

His frown deepened. "Poppy, you shouldn't have left the house on your own."

She responded by flashing him a smile. "I'm not on my own. I have two gentlemen here to escort me into town."

Dr. Carmichael shook his head and grinned again. "I'm afraid I shall have to leave you now. Lord Welles, how is Lady Lavinia? I know she usually struggles when it rains as heavily as it did this morning."

Poppy responded before Nathaniel had the chance. "She wasn't feeling well, slow to get out of bed this morning, but she dressed and came downstairs around eleven. Would you look in on her? She did seem a little paler than usual."

"Then I shall do so." He cast her a smile and nodded toward Nathaniel before hopping the stone fence with the agile strength of a young boy, using it as a shortcut to the manor house.

Poppy resumed walking, quickening her strides to keep ahead of Nathaniel, but he was taller and his legs were longer. He caught up to her with little difficulty. She was the one breathing harder to maintain the brisk pace.

"Why are you so overset?" he asked. "You know Thad and Penelope can't help but bicker. I think they enjoy it."

"I know, but our earlier talk affected me more than I realized."

"I was afraid of that." He placed her arm in his and slowed her pace as they continued to walk to town. "It was a difficult discussion and not fair of me to impose my problems on you."

She looked up at him. "No, Nathaniel. I'm glad you did. It was just a bit much for me to take in all at once. My life has been so sheltered. I've never endured hardship or faced the possibility of death in battle. We lost one of our relatives in the war, my father's cousin, Harrison Farthingale. It devastated the family. I cannot comprehend losing as many dear friends as you have lost."

She cast him a hesitant smile. "In truth, this walk helped me. Dr. Carmichael came along, and he was on his way back from visiting Mrs. Fitch. Do you know her son, Walter? He sprained his wrist."

"I know him, and I've heard talk of your connection to him." He looked at her in admiration, a precious look that she'd treasure forever. But this was Nathaniel's strength. He encouraged her to take on challenges. He never felt threatened or overshadowed by the women in his family. "I haven't heard the full story. Tell me about it while we walk."

"Mrs. Fitch was right about here with her young children when Walter suddenly decided to make his appearance. Penelope, Olivia, and I happened along and saw her struggling." She quickly told him the rest of it. "So there I was, holding her hand and assuring her all would be well, when Walter's head emerged. My heart stopped. I didn't know what to do next, but Dr. Carmichael came along just then and handled everything."

"You were beside her when it mattered."

"I was at hand, that's all."

He regarded her thoughtfully. "It must have been a proud moment for you."

"It was," she admitted. "But it was also an odd summer. Unsettling in many ways, not only because of Walter's unexpected arrival." She took a deep breath and continued. "I was fourteen at the time. You were still off fighting in the war. Your father was ill, but Lavinia refused to break with tradition. Penelope would have her friends visit her no matter what else was going on with the family."

"I'm glad you were there for my sister."

She nodded. "It was a hard time for her. Your mother had passed, and now your father was in failing health. The brother she adored," she said, referring to him, "was off somewhere on a foreign battlefield. She didn't know whether you were dead or alive. Goose and I did our best to cheer her up that summer. We made a pact. We were never going to abandon Penelope in her time of need. We had no idea when we walked into town that summer day Mrs. Fitch would also be in need."

When she finished telling him the story, he stopped a moment and tucked a finger under her chin to draw her gaze to his. "The world needs more kind hearts such as yours. Don't ever change, Poppy. Nor ever believe you have nothing to offer. You have an extraordinary ability to heal wounded hearts."

He slipped his hand away. "But let's have no more serious discussions. Only pleasant chatter for the rest of the day. I'll buy you a lemonade, and you can tell me all about the man of your dreams. I want to hear your list."

"Ah, I see. Turnabout is fair play?"

She squinted into the sun as she looked up at him again, for the clouds were quickly disappearing and there were even more blue patches in the sky. The warm air still felt moist, and she breathed in the earthy scent of wet wood and muddy ground, and in the mix was the subtle scent of Nathaniel's sandalwood soap.

"Yes. How am I to help you find the right man unless I know more about your likes and dislikes?" He shook his head and laughed lightly as they continued down the road. He had a nice laugh, deep and mellow. Genuinely pleasing to her ears. "Of course, since you are far more clever than I am, you probably don't need my help. Still, it is my responsibility to keep you away from the rakes who will lead you to ruin."

"My, that's awfully severe. I'm not a witless fool. I don't intend to run off to Gretna Green with the first man who smiles at me."

"Perhaps I'm being a little dramatic. But your happiness is important to me, I hope you know that. A man doesn't need to have wicked designs on you to still be wrong for you. *The Book of Love's* author claims that a woman's brain is different from that of the male. I don't know that we are so very different. Once the male gets past the initial urge to spill his seed far and wide, aren't we then looking for the same thing? The connections that will make for a happy union."

She nodded. "I suppose."

"So, you must make your list. What qualities do you wish for in a husband?"

She tipped her head up and smiled at him. "Do you want to hear them now or must I write them down and show them to you later?"

"Now. I'm too curious to wait. Besides, I know you've given more thought to it than I ever gave to choosing a wife. Shows what an idiot I am. But you have a good head on your shoulders. What are your required qualities?"

"Oh, you know. The usual."

"What? Incredibly handsome. Wealthy. Titled?"

She skipped over a few puddles in the road. "All those things are optional. He must be utterly devoted to me and our children. A family man."

"Family is important to you."

"Yes, of course. I couldn't be with someone who shunted his children aside while he made the rounds of parties and entertainments every evening. Not that I would expect him to become a recluse, but there must be a balance that tips in favor of his family."

She avoided another puddle and continued. "He must be thoughtful, but also have a sense of humor. He must be kind. I know it is fashionable to be considered a gentleman, but such a man holds little appeal for me. The men in my family are hard workers. I don't know that I could respect a man who wakes at noon and does nothing all day. That isn't for me, no matter how handsome or wealthy he is. No matter if he has a title."

"It always struck me as odd, as well. Why think more of a man because he idles the day away? I'm glad you weren't taken in by that. You truly are quite sensible."

She shook her head and laughed. "I am going to memorialize your statement by writing it down in my diary. Lord Welles declared me to be sensible today. I don't believe that statement has ever been made of a Farthingale before."

He emitted a hearty chuckle.

"I know you meant it as a compliment, but a young woman with good sense is not considered desirable in Society. Wealth and status are the highly prized traits. Which is precisely why I haven't made a very good impression in my first Season."

"Not everyone does. It signifies nothing."

"I don't know that I will ever be comfortable making the rounds of balls and soirees. I find most of the ballroom chatter quite dull, and I'm not very good at batting my eyelashes and giggling inanely at jests that I do not find funny at all."

Nathaniel nodded. "You surprise me. I still think of you, Goose, and Penelope as those ten-year-old girls who used to chatter and giggle in those long-ago summers. But you've grown up. I like those little girls you were. Joyful and innocent. But I also like the women you've become."

She sighed wistfully. "Things are changing. Goose is married now. I expect Penelope will marry soon. It will hurt to lose my best friends. Oh, we'll always remain dearest friends, but they'll have their own households to run and children to raise."

"So will you when you marry. Are there any men who have caught your attention?"

You, you, you. But she could never admit this to him now. "Do you mean in London? Not really."

"Well then, how about here in Wellesford?"

"There aren't too many. Although the vicar, Adam Carstairs, and the doctor, Angus Carmichael, are good men. I'd mention Andrew Gordon, but it will put you in a temper. What is it about him you don't like?"

"Plenty."

"Such as?"

"He's a peacock in a uniform. He struts and preens but there is no substance to him. Only surface glitter and little more to him than that."

"That is odd. I've spoken to him and he seems to be quite intelligent."

Nathaniel snorted. "He's a codswallop."

"What does that mean?"

Nathaniel ran a hand across the nape of his neck, obviously tense and cross. His nostrils flared and his eyes turned stormy. "It means you're to stay away from him. It means that if I see him approaching you, I'll–"

She laughed. "Nathaniel, do you hear yourself? You sound like one of those dominant male baboons my cousin, Lily, is always going on about. I am not one of the female baboons in your troop. You cannot chase away the other males who wish to sniff me."

He emitted a low, feral growl that surprised her by its sensuality.

A ripple of excitement shot through her.

A hot ripple, in truth. The flecks of gray in Nathaniel's eyes were like burning embers, fiery and smoldering. His chest was puffed out and he looked as though he might start beating on it at any moment, pounding out a possessive tune. *Mine. You are mine. Only I shall ever sniff you.*

Her eyes widened as she stared at him.

Was it possible?

Is he jealous?

No, it isn't possible.

Dear heaven, it can't happen.

He had to fall in love with Charlotte, for she was carrying his child. How could there be any other outcome to this situation?

Chapter Six

Nathaniel's heart slammed into his chest. Not once. Not twice. But repeatedly. Hard punches that had him reeling. What was it about Poppy? Her smile struck him like a body blow. Her slightest touch seared his soul.

He ached just looking at her.

And yet, he also felt wrapped in warmth when looking at her. Those big, blue eyes of hers were glorious pools, perhaps a gentle stream that carried you along in its soothing current.

But there was nothing gentle about his feelings for the girl. He was suddenly a possessive brute.

Only he would ever touch her.

Only he would ever kiss her.

Only he would ever wrap her in his arms and fill her.

Lord help him! What was he thinking?

He stepped away from Poppy and turned his back to her, needing a moment to regain control of his traitorous body. Even turned away, he could *feel* her beside him. Every one of his senses was screaming and churning within him.

He made the mistake of looking at her again.

A breeze blew gently through her dark curls. It billowed and swirled around her gown so that the fabric flowed and clung to her long, slender legs and her hips. Her gown was lavender, and that made him think of her scent, for it was also lavender. He wanted to taste it on her skin. He wanted to capture her lips in a long, lingering kiss.

The worst of it was that he suddenly wanted to hold her close to his heart, take her into his heart. Keep her there always and protect her. Love her. Raise a family with her.

It was madness.

No doubt a case of sunstroke. "Poppy, I–"

"Don't say it, Nathaniel. Don't say anything. Go home. I'll find someone in town to escort me back to the house when I finish my errands."

He ran a hand raggedly through his hair. "No, I don't want you walking there alone. And who will you ask to escort you back?"

She rolled her eyes. "I'll look for the most untrustworthy scoundrel I can find and ask him."

He ignored her sarcasm. "I'll send my carriage for you. The driver will wait beside the Golden Hart."

"Very well. I won't be long."

He watched her until she'd walked into town, still not liking that she was there on her own. But everyone from the local baker, to the bookshop owner, to the farrier would notice her presence and run out to protect her if anything untoward were to happen.

At the moment, he was the greatest danger to her.

What's worse, she knew it.

He hadn't been able to mask his hunger for her.

He glanced up, scowling heavenward. "Lord, why do this to me?"

He'd known the girl all of her life. Suddenly, she'd become the woman of his dreams. Was this real? Or his way of rebelling against the problems piled on his shoulders. And now Charlotte Winthrow was to visit.

"Lord Welles, is anything wrong?" Dr. Carmichael was just walking out the door as he returned to Sherbourne.

"No, distracted by my thoughts is all. How is my aunt?"

The doctor smiled. "She's holding up nicely. Merely a touch

of lumbago. She'll be in the pink by the time the Duke of Winthrow and his daughter arrive. Your aunt invited me to the dinner party you're hosting in their honor."

Nathaniel shook his head and laughed. "I'm hosting a dinner party? Yes, of course. I leave such matters to Lavinia and Penelope. They are far more capable than I am when it comes to arranging parties. You are always welcome, Carmichael. Did they mention when the party is to be held?"

"Saturday evening. I think half the town will be invited."

"Is that so? My sister's idea, no doubt." He needed to speak to Penelope before she put whatever diabolical plans to thwart a marriage between him and Charlotte into action. There would be no marriage between them, but it irked him that his sister was meddling in his life, determined to impose her will on his happiness. And it irked him that he liked Poppy and was turning into a panting dog, unable to stem his lust for her.

It irked him most that his sister had been right about Poppy being perfect for him.

And since he was already out of joint, it irked him that Penelope was constantly bickering with Thad. "Well then, I'll see you Saturday evening."

When the doctor left, Nathaniel went in search of Penelope and found her in the parlor. She was seated beside their aunt, both of them hovered over an invitation list. Ah, these glorious lists that everyone made. He often made lists when dealing with his business affairs. It was efficient. It was logical.

He was growing to hate them. There was nothing wrong with tossing caution to the wind and ripping up all lists. No one adhered to them anyway, least of all him. He'd done a miserable job of describing Charlotte. A sad state of affairs since he knew her intimately. Or rather, he'd been intimate with her, but hardly knew her at all. He wasn't about to make a list of what had led to that fateful evening or what he'd done. It would have shocked Poppy. Fortunately, no harm had come of it.

Still, how could he have been so stupid? But all his defenses had been stripped that evening, for he'd earlier been to the docks and seen those coffins lined up. Friends lost forever.

Get drunker than you have ever been in your life.

Continue drinking when you reach Lord Angstrom's ball.

Ignore the alarm bells when Lady Charlotte suggestively lays her hand on your thigh while you are seated beside her at the dinner table.

Agree to meet her in Lord Angstrom's conservatory, and when you do, don't bother to talk. Just lift up her gown and drop your pants.

Take care to pull out before spilling your seed inside of her.

Try to remember her name when she slips away to return to the ball.

Remember to button your trousers.

Indeed, such a list should have sobered him quickly, but he'd simply returned to the ball and guzzled more champagne, trying to forget those boxes filled with precious souls. And now he had to find a way to make amends to Charlotte because he was not going to marry her. "Penelope, you can't invite the entire town of Wellesford to the dinner party. You know the Duke of Winthrow will not like rubbing elbows with our neighbors."

She stiffened and shot him an indignant look. "Then he ought to go home if he doesn't enjoy our rustic hospitality."

"And take his daughter with him? That isn't going to happen." He frowned, knowing she was going to make life hell for him until he came to his senses and chose Poppy. "Who else besides Dr. Carmichael have you invited? Let me look at your list."

He struck off most of the names, leaving only the doctor, Vicar Carstairs, the Plimptons, and unfortunately, their idiot nephew, Andrew Gordon. Beast and Goose were invited, of course. Thad and Poppy since they were guests in his home.

"We must invite more families. There are more men than ladies, and everyone knows you must have an equal number at the table or the party will be deemed an utter failure."

"Penelope, that is nonsense. Then don't invite the vicar or Captain Gordon."

She rolled her eyes. "I cannot rule them out. Don't you know anything about anything?"

He shot his sister a murderous look. "Apparently, I don't."

Lavinia sighed. "Invite Lord Lothbridge and his daughters. They are of suitable age. That will even out our table. I think it's an excellent list. Lord Lothbridge will be pleased to have these fine gentlemen present. Deandra is his eldest and quite pretty. Too pretty to be considered a spinster. Perhaps one of these gentlemen will take a fancy to her."

Goose, who had been reading in a corner, came over to join them. "I'll play some lively tunes afterward, so we'll have music for those who wish to dance. It will be a perfect party, Lavinia. Not too big. Not too small. The Duke of Winthrow and his daughter cannot find fault with it."

"But they will anyway," Penelope muttered.

There were times when Nathaniel wanted to wring his sister's neck. She was like a dog with a bone that she would not let go. "Don't think to set Pip loose on Charlotte. It's you I'll take to the woodshed and thrash if he drops a spider into her teacup."

"Honestly, Nathaniel. You cannot think to–"

"Enough, Penelope!" He was in no humor for her insolence at the moment.

The duke and his daughter would be on their doorstep in a matter of days. Lavinia's blackmailer would surely strike, and he had no idea who the man was… or even if it was a man. Nor did he know the whereabouts of Lavinia's baby who was all grown up now. Perhaps the child was the blackmailer.

"Charlotte Winthrow is a–"

"Watch what you say about her! She will be my wife, assuming she accepts my offer of marriage. Get used to it. She will soon be your sister." *Lord,* why had he blurted that lie?

Penelope ran out in tears.

"Oh, dear." Goose hurried after her.

Lavinia was too old to sprint out of the parlor, so she simply took out her handkerchief and dabbed the tears forming in her eyes. "Poor Poppy. She'll be devastated."

"Why should Poppy care?" Of course, he knew the girl adored him. They'd always gotten along well. But whatever respect or affection she harbored for him was now dead.

"She's been in love with you ever since she first set eyes on you."

"Lavinia, she was a child. I assure you, she does not love me now." Indeed, he hoped she had more sense than that. *Yes*, she did have more sense. Wasn't this what his earlier discussion with Poppy had been about? Her common sense.

Her healing touch.

He'd poured out his heart to her concerning the war, revealing his innermost pain. It had wrung him dry. He was obviously still out of sorts, or he would never have lashed out at Penelope the way he had done.

Lavinia shook her head and sighed. "You don't stop loving someone simply because it is convenient to do so."

He stared at his aunt. Was it possible she still loved the man who had ruined her? He needed to find out more about him. But how was he to start the conversation? He'd ask Poppy. She would know. She would do anything to protect Lavinia.

Thad and Beast strode in.

"What's going on?" Beast asked. "Penelope rushed past us in tears, and Goose was too busy chasing after her to stop and tell us."

Nathaniel ran a hand across the back of his neck and groaned. "Nothing. Just putting together a list for Saturday night's dinner party."

Thad arched an eyebrow. "Och, must be some list."

Nathaniel nodded. "Hell of a list."

Beast slapped him on the shoulder. "You look like you could use a drink. How about we three walk to the Golden Hart?"

"No, I've sent my carriage into town and the driver is to wait there for Poppy. She won't be keen on seeing me just now. But I'll take you up on the offer once she returns."

Thad's eyebrow shot up again. "Poppy is mad at you, too?

She never loses her temper at anyone. What the hell did you do?"

Nathaniel frowned. "Nothing."

"Oh, you did something," Thad remarked with a laugh. "Did you try to kiss her?"

"No."

Beast muffled his laughter with a cough. "Maybe she's angry because you didn't kiss her. You're her test frog, after all. Perhaps her test failed."

Nathaniel rolled his eyes in exasperation. "No test. No failure. No idea what got her so overset. Drop it."

Thad patted him on the back. "Well, it's as I've always said. Big girls. Big problems."

Beast nodded. "This is going to be a fun party."

Nathaniel groaned. "Hell of a party."

Chapter Seven

Nathaniel. Test frog. Day Three.
Earls make terrible test frogs.

POPPY WAS LATE coming down to breakfast the following morning, hoping to avoid everyone. Apparently, everyone had the same idea, for all were now seated around the table, just about to dig into their food.

The silence as she walked in was deafening.

Pip was the only cheerful one. "We're to have more company on Friday, and a dinner party on Saturday," Pip said, knocking over his glass of milk as she settled in the chair beside him. "Bollocks! I didn't mean to do it. I swear."

Poppy shot out of her chair and quickly righted his glass, then set her table linen over the spill to sop it up before it dripped onto the floor. She moved aside as one of the footmen properly attended to it. "Oh, Pip."

"I'm so sorry, Poppy." His smile crumbled and he looked as though he was about to cry.

She quickly forgave him, for there had been enough tears spilled this past day, along with this morning's milk. She couldn't bear to see another sad face. "It's all right. We are all off stride this morning."

The men looked hungover. One would think Pip had exploded a cannonball in their ears, the way they'd cringed and moaned in response to the light *thunk* of the glass as it fell over on the table.

Penelope's eyes were red and swollen. She must have cried herself to sleep last night and cried some more this morning. Lavinia and Goose were nursing headaches, no doubt a result of dealing with Penelope and the men.

Even Periwinkle had his paws over his eyes and his head bowed as he sat on Lavinia's lap.

Was it wrong of her to hope the Duke of Winthrow and his daughter would be abducted by pirates and put on a ship sailing to the opposite end of the world?

She supposed it wouldn't do.

Nathaniel looked like the Grim Reaper.

His aunt and sister looked as though they were about to burst into tears again.

"Well, isn't this charming," she muttered. "What a jolly party."

Pip, who had resumed his seat now that his milk spill had been cleaned up, was the only one to laugh at her mirthless jest. "Oh, Poppy. You got a letter. I saw it sitting on the salver in the entry hall. Did Soames give it to you yet?"

"No, I've only just come down."

Pip hopped to his feet again, this time almost knocking over her cup of tea. "Oops, sorry. I'll get the letter for you. It isn't from your sister or your parents."

Nathaniel frowned at the boy. "Sit down, Pip. Leave Poppy alone and stop snooping. The letter is none of your business."

"But I always snoop. You don't usually catch me at it." He grinned and ran off to fetch the letter.

Poppy inspected it when Pip handed it to her. She did not recognize the handwriting either. "Hmm, there's no indication of who wrote it." Since no one was talking anyway, she decided to open it at the table. It was considered rude to do so, but everyone was out of sorts this morning and it was a short letter.

Pip must have been reading it over her shoulder, for he suddenly burst out laughing. "It's a love letter. Poppy has a secret admirer! Poppy has a secret admirer!" He brought his hand up to his lips and began to make crude kissing noises.

"Stop that, Pip," she said in a sharp whisper.

The three men looked on, saying nothing but obviously stunned. The ladies looked delighted.

"Let me see the letter." Nathaniel rose to his full height and reached across the table to grab it.

"No, it's mine." Poppy held it protectively away from him.

Nathaniel was getting that big baboon beating on his chest look again. "It's a *love* letter. Delivered to my home. Let me see it."

"It was delivered to *me*," she corrected.

"What coward would write to you and not reveal his name?" He came around to her side of the table and took the seat next to hers. His brow was furrowed and he did not look pleased. Wordlessly, he held out his hand.

"Very well," she grumbled, handing it over to him.

His nearness was making the butterflies in her stomach spark to life. When she breathed him in, she caught the scent of sandalwood and lather from his recent shave. It was subtly seductive and arousing, just as *The Book of Love* described. She wanted to melt into his arms and put her lips to his neck to kiss him the way Pip had mimicked only moments ago.

Yes, she wanted to slobber him with kisses.

"This isn't even original," he said with a feral growl. "This is a Shakespeare sonnet. Shall I compare thee to a summer's day? Thou art more lovely… what the hell?" He read a few more lines, sounding like a growling wolf as he recited them rather than a respected earl of the realm. "He ends it with *your ardent and devoted admirer, A.C.*"

He frowned at her as though it was her fault she had a secret beau.

Thad stared at him. "Well, the coward put his initials on it, so perhaps we can guess who it is. A.C. The doctor perhaps? Angus Carmichael."

"Or the vicar," Beast said, adding his opinion. "Adam Carstairs. He does seem to smile a lot in Poppy's presence."

Nathaniel stared at it again. "It could be A.G. Andrew Gordon. Bollocks. I'll rip him apart if he comes near you, Poppy."

She sighed. "No, Nathaniel. You won't do any such thing."

Penelope was staring at him through her reddened eyes. "Why would you rip him apart?" She gasped. "Because he likes Poppy and you're jealous?"

He raked a hand through his hair. "I'm not jealous. He's a dolt. An arse. A pretentious–"

Pip burst out laughing. "You said arse!"

"Be quiet, Pip, or I'll feed you to Periwinkle." He turned back to Poppy, his frown deepening. "He is not a suitable husband for you."

"Your opinion has been duly noted." She tried to keep the irritation from her voice but failed.

Perhaps she wasn't being fair to him. He did not love her, but he was worried about her. Why did he detest Captain Gordon? He liked the other possible admirers well enough. He'd made no comment about the doctor or the vicar. They were good men and he knew it, although he'd made feeble excuses about their unsuitability the other day.

But his dislike of Captain Gordon was something altogether different.

She was worried. If these two men were left alone together, blood would be spilled. Not serious blood, of course. Perhaps a bloody lip or bloodied knuckles.

Beast arched an eyebrow as he stared at her, his black eyepatch prominent and making him look quite dangerous. "Poppy, are you all right?"

"No. I've never had a beau before." Suddenly, everything she'd learned from *The Book of Love* flew out of her head. "What am I supposed to do?"

"Do?" Nathaniel repeated with a soft growl "You are to do nothing. Come to me immediately if you receive another letter from that coward."

"And you're going to help her?" Penelope retorted. "What will your precious Charlotte think of that?"

Poppy felt her heart give a little rip.

She adored Penelope, but did her friend not realize she was pouring salt on Poppy's deep and open wound?

"POPPY, GET THE book and join me in my study once you've finished breakfast," Nathaniel said, gentling his voice as he spoke to her. He cast a warning glance around the table to make certain no one would comment. They all kept silent, as he expected they would. They'd given their opinions on his making a love match with Poppy.

His sister had been most vocal about it, but everyone seated at the breakfast table loved Poppy and would consider him the biggest dolt ever to walk the earth if he did not marry her.

He didn't give a rat's tail what any of them thought.

He would fall in love at his own pace, at a time of his own choosing, and with a girl of his choosing. If that girl happened to be Poppy, so be it.

But it would be *his* choice, made with due deliberation.

He wasn't going to recklessly jump in and spout mad, impetuous declarations of love to anyone. Certainly not before the matter of Lavinia was settled.

Poppy nodded and rose to leave, but he put his hand over hers to hold her back. "Have your breakfast first. You look like you need reinforcement. Meet me there whenever you're ready."

She nodded again and then stared at their hands because his still lay atop hers.

Damn.

He had no desire to remove it, but he did so before everyone noticed and deigned it their duty to comment.

Why did her hand have to be so soft and perfect? It was the

sort of hand one could hold onto forever.

He cleared his throat and was about to pour himself another cup of coffee to take into his study, when Soames entered. "My lord, Dr. Carmichael is here to see Lady Lavinia."

"Speak of the devil." Thad snorted. "Send him in, Soames."

Beast chuckled as he nodded. "Yes, at once."

Soames, ever loyal, awaited Nathaniel's reply. He wanted to tell his butler to shoot the bounder and feed his carcass to the dogs. But he supposed that would not do. "Lady Lavinia will see him in the parlor. Send him there."

"Don't be silly. Have him join us, Soames," Lavinia insisted. "I'll see him right here."

Nathaniel sighed. "Very well. Bring him in." If the doctor was Poppy's secret admirer, he wanted to know it sooner rather than later. Indeed, it was obvious everyone at the table wanted to know it.

"My apologies," Dr. Carmichael said, walking in with a smile on his face that faded as he noticed everyone gawking at him. "It, um… it appears I've come at a bad time."

"Not at all," Lavinia intoned. "Do join us. Have you had your breakfast?"

"Yes, hours ago. I only stopped in to see how you were feeling. Any better?"

Lavinia smiled. "Yes, much better. The pains have gone. We were just speaking of Shakespeare."

"Ah, England's jewel in the crown. One of my favorites, but I suppose he is everyone's favorite." Despite being offered a seat, he remained standing just inside the doorway, his faded smile now turning into a frown as they all continued to stare at him. "My lady, if you are feeling well, then I'll be on my way."

"What is your favorite work of his?" Nathaniel asked, hoping to sound casual, but the question sounded like a Spanish inquisition even to his own ears.

"Of Shakespeare's?" The doctor began to fidget with his collar. "I don't think I have one in particular. Perhaps Macbeth, since it is the Scottish play, and I'm a Scot, as you all know. My lord, I hope you won't find me rude, but what is going on? Why are you all looking at me as though I've grown a third eye in the center of my forehead?"

Nathaniel ignored the question. He was the one conducting this interrogation. "Do you enjoy his sonnets?"

"Dare I respond? You look ready to hang me if I give the wrong answer." He crossed his arms over his chest, prepared to wait Nathaniel out, but then sighed. "Yes, I enjoy them. Shall I compare thee to a summer's day… however, I prefer his plays. What's this about?"

Nathaniel held out Poppy's letter. "Did you write this?"

Dr. Carmichael perused it, then his eyes widened when he noticed the initials. "Miss Farthingale, rest assured, I did not! Were I to court you… first of all, I would never consider it. A country doctor? Aspiring to marry you? The notion is absurd."

Poppy blushed to her roots.

"It is not absurd at all," Lavinia said. "Poppy, you are lovely. I'm sure every man in town is a little in love with you. Do sit down, Dr. Carmichael. We did not mean to put you on the spot."

He laughed. "Oh, Lord Welles certainly did. Were I of a higher station, Miss Farthingale, I would be following you about like a faithful hound. The man you choose to marry will be fortunate, indeed. But this letter was not written by me."

He ignored Nathaniel's glower and studied Poppy thoughtfully. "My handwriting is atrocious. I'm not one to toss about elegant words, either. Especially not poetic ones. And I'd sign my name to any letter I wrote, not hide behind some fake initials." He turned to Lavinia. "Are you truly feeling well?"

She chuckled. "Yes, doctor. I am."

"Then I shall be on my way. I'll see you all on Saturday, assuming I'm still invited."

Nathaniel nodded. "Of course, you are. Forgive my ill temper."

"Nothing to forgive, my lord. I know you take your responsibilities seriously." But he was shaking his head and chuckling as he left them.

Poppy was still blushing, and now struggling to hold back tears. Nathaniel silently kicked himself for his callousness. He'd turned the matter of the letter into a circus. Perhaps Goose or Penelope would not have minded so much, but Poppy was more reserved. She did not like to boast about herself or have others fuss over her.

Indeed, she had no idea how beautiful she was inside and out.

It amazed him she did not recognize her spectacular allure. "Poppy, I'm sorry. I handled this badly. It just seemed too much of a coincidence that Angus Carmichael should stop by so soon after you received this letter. I don't like that your admirer is playing coy."

"He did write his initials."

"He was hiding behind those initials knowing there are half a dozen men in town with the same ones. Perhaps more, because we can't tell if his last name begins with a C or a G. Perhaps it's a sloppily written O or Q. Not that it matters. The point is, he's hiding, and I don't like it."

"Nor do I," Beast said. "Think of what happened to Goose. I don't want anyone attempting to abduct you."

Poppy tensed. "Abduction? The possibility hadn't crossed my mind."

Great, now they'd scared her.

Nathaniel gazed at the letter. Was it possible the person who'd written it was the blackmailer? He needed to compare the handwriting to the one Lavinia had received. "May I hold onto it for now?"

Poppy emitted a ragged sigh and nodded.

"No harm will come to you." He placed his hand over hers again. "You're safe here. We are merely considering all the possibilities, no matter how remote. You know I will protect you. Thad and Beast will do the same. So will Pip." He grinned at his young cousin and saw the pride of responsibility shine in the boy's eyes.

Pip noticed things that adults overlooked. Perhaps he'd figure out the identity of Poppy's admirer before any of them could. "So, take a deep breath. Finish your breakfast and then come to me."

He gave a curt nod and retired to his study.

Beast and Thad excused themselves from the table and followed him, leaving the women to chat among themselves. "Do ye believe the lass is in danger?" Thad asked, closing the door behind him.

"I don't know. Likely, it's just a letter and the besotted dolt will declare himself soon. Or he'll be too afraid to act on his feelings and just slither away like the lowly snake he is."

"Not rushing to judgement, are you?" Thad teased.

"If you're worried for her safety, then do what I did to protect Goose," Beast said, settling into one of the leather chairs beside his desk.

"Marry her? First of all, the danger to Goose was real. Second of all, you were in love with her and just looking for any excuse to marry her without having to admit you loved her. Bachelors are such cowards. We're all the same. Believing we are somehow made lesser by revealing what's in our heart."

Thad strode to the window and casually leaned his shoulder against the wall as he peered out. "Are you saying you don't love Poppy?"

"I love all three of them. Don't you? They are an important part of our lives. They are the reminder that sweetness and innocence can thrive in a dark world. But I'm not going to marry her simply because everyone wishes it."

Beast softly grumbled. "You're not serious about marrying Charlotte Winthrow, are you?"

Nathaniel raked a hand through his hair as he settled in his chair behind his desk. "Of course not. I said that to rile Penelope because she was going on about Charlotte's unworthiness like a rabid dog. I didn't know how else to shut her up. I suppose I ought to apologize to her, but I want to let her stew a little while longer. Are all sisters this irritating?"

Thad chuckled as he turned to him. "All siblings are. I think it's required."

Nathaniel grunted. "What do you think of this love letter Poppy received? Am I needlessly worrying about it?"

"Perhaps," Thad said, "but one can't be too careful. I know it isn't the same as Goose's situation, but why not be sure? I think I'll pay a call on the vicar. I've noticed his gaze straying to Poppy during his sermon. Might as well do some productive investigation while I'm here."

Nathaniel nodded. "Just don't scare the man. The townspeople like him and won't be pleased if we chase him away, especially if he didn't write it." He joined his friend beside the window and put a hand on his shoulder. "Your regiment will be returning soon. I know you're to meet their ship at Plymouth in a fortnight. Let me know if you'd like company on your journey."

Thad nodded. "I'm grateful for the offer but it won't be necessary."

Nathaniel and Beast exchanged somber glances.

They'd all been through the war, had all faced the loss of friends and family. But Thad's situation had the makings of disaster. The main regimental force had stayed on in France to secure the peace. Only the dead and injured were coming home, and Thad had been assigned to meet that ship. He'd heard nothing more in the weeks since that order was issued, receiving no list of survivors or list of the dead.

"We lost a lot of men at Waterloo," Thad said. "I saw many fall in battle. But Wellington ordered me back to London immediately after the fighting stopped, and I've received no news since. It was chaos when I left. In truth, I don't know what I'm doing back here. There's nothing for me to do but wait, and we all know how patient I am." He cast Nathaniel a mirthless smile. "I had a purpose in the midst of battle. But I'm useless here."

Thad was a captain in the Royal Scots Greys, one of the oldest and finest dragoon cavalry regiments.

Nathaniel frowned. "You and I must have a talk before you leave Sherbourne. I mean it, Thad. It's important. I know what you're going through. I went through the same months ago, before Waterloo, thinking I could handle the task, but it's a very different feeling from accounting for the dead and wounded on a battlefield. I wasn't prepared to meet the ship when it brought my men home. It was those coffins lined up on the dock, you see. Silent. Impersonal. Neatly stacked. It rips you apart."

Nathaniel had lost friends, but it would be worse for Thad. He had brothers and cousins, kinsmen and clansmen, fighting alongside him. How many of them would show up on the lists? It had to be on Thad's mind. Indeed, he was likely obsessed with worry. "Will you allow me to say anything to my sister? She might go easier on you if she knows."

Thad laughed. "No. Loopy is the only thing keeping me sane right now. She pokes and prods, makes me angry, makes me laugh. Makes me feel as though I am still living. She's the blister on my foot that refuses to pop."

"How delightful. I'm sure she'll melt in your arms when she hears those words." Beast rose from his chair, shaking his head and chuckling. "Come on, Thad. I'm sure Goose and Loopy are missing us. Looks like it will be a nice day. Let's walk into town. We'll take Pip with us. Nathaniel, what are you going to say to Poppy?"

"I have no idea."

It wasn't long after his friends left that Poppy appeared at his door. She had *The Book of Love* in hand.

She looked lovely. The soft blue of her gown matched the soft hue of her eyes. Her gowns were always fashionable, but modest. The book's author spoke of the male's lower-brain attraction to the female, which is why men's gazes always strayed to the female breast. Healthy breasts. Fertile female.

Women understood this power and often wore fashions to lure a man's gaze just there.

But Poppy was shy by nature. She would not be comfortable using her sensual appeal to lure a man. Nor did he need her pointing her breasts at him to notice her in that way. To his dismay, he'd long since passed that point with Poppy. "Come in and have a seat."

Well, noticing Poppy as more than his sister's friend wasn't dismaying so much as surprising. She was easy to look at. Beautiful. That's what worried him. She grew more beautiful in his eyes with each passing day. Each encounter.

Hers was a subtle allure that crept up on you and swallowed you whole while you weren't paying attention.

How long before everyone noticed that he was attracted to Poppy?

Thankfully, the Winthrows would arrive soon, and he'd be too occupied entertaining them and his other friends to make a fool of himself over this girl.

Besides, he had not ruled out Charlotte altogether. She was a renowned beauty. Surely, he'd get over this inexplicable fascination with Poppy once Charlotte arrived.

Poppy closed the door, this time showing no hesitation as she settled in the chair opposite his desk.

Since he preferred not put distance between them as they spoke of Poppy's anonymous suitor, he came around to the front of the desk and sat beside her. Instantly, he realized his mistake. The girl was stirring his senses again. He caught the scent of lavender on her warm skin and had the sudden urge to put his lips to the slender curve of her neck and soak in her intoxicating fragrance.

"Nathaniel, the book doesn't say anything about anonymous love letters."

He tore his gaze from hers and pretended to concentrate on the book. "I know. But the author has a good understanding of men, and since it appears you are attracting suitors, you need to be more aware of what's really going on in a man's brain whenever he speaks to you."

She was blushing again, for her cheeks were pink and so were the tips of her ears. "I'm not a simpleton. I understand men have physical urges. Sometimes they're expressed poetically in letters such as these."

"Shakespeare wrote those words. The dolt who copied them is a dim-witted, lazy–"

"Lazy because he could not come up with his own romantic words? Honestly, Nathaniel. You can't condemn a man for that. And you needn't be concerned about my response. It will take more than a few words of flattery to sway me. Give me some credit for being careful."

"I do. You know I think you're clever. And you also know I'm not saying this just to be kind to you."

She nodded.

"What you don't understand is the power of these five senses that are explained in the book. You mentioned to me that you are an observer."

"Yes, but I don't wish to be. I want to experience all these marvelous sensations. Not to the point of tossing caution to the wind, mind you. I intend to be careful, but what if I'm caught off guard and carried away in the moment? I need to know what to expect."

Nathaniel cleared his throat.

The thought of Poppy being carried away with passion ought to have made him laugh. Instead, it just made him hot and curious.

"This letter, for example," she continued, unaware that he was struggling not to think of her in any mindless, low-brained way. "How do I know when a man's affection is real and when it is feigned? Should I trust my instincts? Should I trust my response? What if I'm swept away by a bounder who only wants me for dishonorable purposes?"

"You can always talk to me." He arched an eyebrow, trying to keep his tone light and manner calm, but Poppy in the throes of passion was not a notion he could get out of his mind. Indeed, he couldn't stop thinking of it to the point of obsession.

Only with me, of course. And no one else. Ever.

He'd kill any man who hurt Poppy.

He'd kill any man who touched Poppy.

Perhaps it was a small overreaction.

She rolled her eyes. "Nathaniel, I don't want talk. I don't want to observe. I want to jump in and gain this knowledge through experience. So, will you?"

"Will I what?"

She frowned at him. "Must I say it?"

He shook his head, clueless. He rarely felt this way, completely at sea and certain he'd missed something important in their conversation. "Yes, I'm afraid you must."

Now even her nose was pink as she said, "I would like you to kiss me. Just once and never again, because I understand your situation and I will never, ever impose on you like this after today. I know the request is impertinent. But I've given it quite a bit of thought and the problem is... well, if you don't kiss me now, then it will never happen and I'll never know."

"Know what exactly?"

She rolled her eyes. "How it feels to be perfectly kissed. You do kiss well, don't you?"

Chapter Eight

NATHANIEL TRIED TO keep his jaw from dropping open. "Poppy, are you asking me to kiss you?"

She blushed furiously, her cheeks a bright, apple red. "I believe I just did. Repeatedly. How much plainer can I be?" They were still seated beside each other. He had only to lean forward and tip his head toward hers. "It seems an important first step, don't you think?"

A dangerous first step.

No, it can't happen.

"What do you think is the second step?" he asked, feeling his throat constricting and irritated that this girl held any power over his heart.

She licked her lips. "I don't know. I haven't gotten past the first. I hadn't considered there would be a second. Why are you being so dense?"

"I'm being protective. Why are you so determined to be ruined?"

Her eyes widened and she gasped. "With a simple kiss? With a man I trust?"

"Have you learned nothing from *The Book of Love*? No, Poppy. You cannot trust me. My thoughts about you are not fatherly in the least. Which is why I know exactly what the scoundrel who wrote you this letter is thinking. And by the way, every man is a scoundrel."

She pursed her lips. "You aren't."

"Are you not listening? I am male."

She cast him a disbelieving glance. "And that makes you a scoundrel?"

"Yes, and more dangerous than the others because you trust me."

"Shouldn't I trust you?"

He ran a hand across the back of his neck. Why were they having this conversation? "Yes, of course you should. But only so far."

She gazed down at the book again and began to leaf through its pages.

"The book won't tell you when to trust me and when to run away from me. Let me give you an example." He reached for her hand. "If I were to take your hand and hold it, you would not be greatly alarmed."

She nodded, staring at his actions as he swallowed her hand in both of his. "What is going through your mind now, Poppy?"

She sighed. "That it feels lovely."

Yes, damn it. It did.

"Warm and comforting," she elaborated.

He let go of her hand, ignoring his own disappointment in releasing her. "But would you still trust me if I were to place my hands on your body and begin to unlace your gown?"

She gasped. "Nathaniel, that's a shocking thing to say. But if *you* were to do it? Of course, I'd trust you."

He groaned and shook his head in exasperation. "No, Poppy. You are missing the point entirely. If a man smiles at you. If a man bows over your hand. If a man takes your hand. If a man does any of these things, what he is telling you is, *I want to put my hands on your body and strip you out of your gown.*"

She swallowed hard and gave a little *eep*.

"Need I describe the rest of what he really wants to do?"

She flipped open the book again and began to search through the chapters. "Oh, it must be here. Where is it?"

"What are you looking for?"

"The answer." She was creating a breeze off the pages as she shuffled through them with obvious desperation.

"Poppy, stop." He put his hands on hers again to still them. "I just told you the answer. Don't ever trust any man. It's as simple as that."

"That isn't my question."

He frowned, not sure what she was going on about. "What is your question?"

She took a deep breath and then another. "What if... now don't be angry with me. But what if I want to let him unlace my gown?"

The thought of putting his hands all over Poppy's luscious body as he peeled her out of–

His heart exploded.

His vision blurred.

He felt a tug to his chest and feared his lungs had exploded, too.

"Nathaniel? Why are you looking at me so oddly?"

He shot to his feet and brought her up along with him. Was she purposely trying to rattle his bones? She'd done an excellent job of it. He was shaken, stomped, tipped upside down, and then shaken some more before being hurled off a cliff. "Poppy, no. The answer is no. If this man loves you, he will refuse you."

"Why?"

"The privilege is for a husband to claim. If this man loves you, he will offer to marry you before he takes you. He'll protect you from this foolishness because he cares for your happiness more than he cares to satisfy his own urges. More than he cares for his own life."

"I see." But her lips were still pursed in a tempting pout, and she did not appear pleased by his response. "If this man loves me, would he not attempt to claim at least one kiss?"

"Why do you insist on making this conversation about kisses?"

"Why are you so adamant that it shouldn't be? What is so terrible about the simple act? Shouldn't I know whether I would enjoy it? Or at least have something to compare it to? It seems foolish to wait until it is too late to fix one's mistake."

She gazed at him, her eyes blazing. "No more lectures, Nathaniel." She pointed to the letter. "If this was sent by Andrew Gordon, then it is likely he will attempt to draw me aside and kiss me at some point during your dinner party. You said it yourself. This is how scoundrels behave. How am I to know the difference between a good kiss and a bad one if I've never experienced one?"

He cleared his throat. "The discussion is over. It is ridiculous."

"Did Olivia have this much trouble with Beast? I'm sure he was a more accommodating test frog." She emitted a soft, ragged breath. "Don't be angry, Nathaniel. You're the only man I trust to be honest with me."

"Kisses lead to other things."

"Like removing one's gown?" She cast him a wry smile. "Which is why I am safest learning these things from you. So, shall we get down to business? You agreed to this, remember? And if Andrew Gordon wrote me this note, then I certainly don't want to trust him with a first kiss."

He groaned, suddenly feeling like a wolf who'd just trapped an innocent lamb. Or was he the lamb suddenly trapped by this beautiful wolf?

No, he was the wolf. He was the worldly, jaded one. So how could he do this to the girl?

Poppy trusted him so completely.

You can do this. You are honorable. You care for her. You will protect her. This is why she chose you to be her first.

"Very well, close your eyes."

She closed them.

He watched them flutter shut. Her dark velvet eyelashes rested against the soft pink of her cheeks.

Blessed Mother. She had the face of an angel.

"What shall I do with my lips?"

He would have laughed at the remark were his heart not too busy erupting with volcanic force within his chest. He was in fiery torment, struggling to hold himself back from devouring Poppy. "Keep them relaxed."

"What shall I do with my hands?"

He dismissed the thought immediately coming to mind, for she would grab the inkpot off his desk and crack his skull open with it if she knew what he was thinking. *Yes*, he was depraved and not proud of it. "Put them on my shoulders." It seemed the safest advice to give her.

"Like this?"

Why did her touch always feel like the touch of heaven?

"It'll do." His voice sounded strained even to his own ears. That she was approaching the kiss with logic ought to have calmed him down.

It didn't.

She was about to ask another question, but he cut her short by wrapping his arms around her and pressing his lips to hers.

He shouldn't have done that.

Nor should he have buried his fingers in her hair and cupped the back of her head to guide her lips to his.

Nor should he have deepened the kiss when she responded, her soft, pliant lips yielding to his possessive conquest. His primitive instincts had taken over. Only his low brain seemed to be working and had taken control.

Her soft, ample breasts molded to his firm chest.

Healthy breasts. Lord, they were healthy.

Mate with this girl.

It was as though she had been built to fit him.

And his low brain knew it. *Fertile female. Want this female. Need to spill seed into this exquisite, beautiful–*

He abruptly pulled his mouth off hers.

Blessed saints! His brain wasn't completely dead yet.

He eased his hold on her. "Well, that's it, Poppy. Your first kiss."

He waited for her to remark on it. Would she think it was magical? Wondrous?

Her eyes remained closed and she said nothing.

He bristled. "Care to comment?"

Poppy had an irritating way of hiding her feelings. She was reserved in everything she said and did. But she hadn't felt reserved in her response to him. The slide of her hands up his chest and the urgent press of her body against his had given her away.

The wild beating of her heart.

He'd felt its rampant beats against his chest.

"Did the kiss meet your expectations?"

She opened her eyes and stared at him. "I'm not sure."

What?

Was this all the response she meant to give him. "What are you not sure about?"

She sighed. "It lacked something."

He shook his head as though he hadn't heard right. "You found my kiss lacking?"

She nodded. "Yes, it lacked conviction."

He'd almost swallowed the girl whole with his throbbing need and pulsing desire. How could she believe he'd kissed her without conviction? He'd held back, to be sure. He hadn't wanted to scare her.

"My gown isn't even askew."

"Your gown? You're complaining because I didn't try to take it off you?" Obviously, he'd been too careful. And who the hell used words such as *askew* when being kissed?

"The point is, my gown isn't so much as rumpled."

"Rumpled?" Is this what she meant? She'd sensed his restraint and mistaken it for lack of caring?

"Nathaniel, would you mind trying it again? But this time, let *your* feelings flow naturally. Allow yourself to feel whatever you would when kissing a woman you desire."

She'd verbally kicked him where it hurt and yet she wanted another kiss?

Of course, he was going to oblige. He was a low-brained male who was not about to pass up the chance to lock lips with a beautiful woman who had a body designed to lead saints into temptation.

He might have been angrier had he not felt the give of her body or seen the soft flush of desire on her cheeks or the satisfied pout on her lips.

Her breaths were still unsteady, he could tell by the rapid rise and fall of her…

Lord, they were beautiful breasts.

He couldn't stop staring at them.

He couldn't stop himself because he was the lowest form of life ever to crawl out of the primordial ooze. He was the lowest of the low-brain males.

"Very well. Let's try this again." He gave her no chance to prepare or draw away, for he meant to give her the no-holding-back kiss she wanted.

His lips descended on hers with possessive hunger.

At the same time, he drew her hard against him so she felt each taut muscle and sinew of his body. He demanded that she yield. He invaded the sweet warmth of her mouth. He unpinned her hair and ran his fingers through her silken curls. He lifted her up so that her lips met his in a crush of wild desire.

He hair tumbled in a silken cascade over his arms and shoulders.

He kissed her long and hard.

He kissed her with his eyes closed. Heart open.

He *tasted* the tea and honey on her lips. Inhaled the *scent* of lavender on her skin. *Heard* her soft moan against his mouth. He knew it would take nothing to undo the ties of her gown. But he wouldn't. It was enough to simply hold her. *Touch* her.

He meant to count to twenty and then release her, but he kept losing count. Finally, he gave up trying and released her gently. "How was it this time?"

Her hair was a glorious tumble and the bodice of her gown was off center so that the swell of one breast was temptingly exposed. He did the unthinkable and bent his head to kiss her there. She gasped and then released her breath in a shaky sigh.

She tried to appear calm and typically reserved, but he saw the look of confused wonder on her face. She smiled, reminding him of a contented kitten on a sun-drenched window seat.

"Nathaniel, will it be like this with Andrew Gordon?"

"Him again?" Her words were a bucket of ice water dumped over his head. But even that blast of ice did nothing to calm the fire burning inside of him. "No, you won't like his kiss. You will never like his kiss. Same goes for any other man."

He picked up the love letter Poppy had received, needing to distract himself from the desire to kiss her again. He was used to women purring and moaning and clawing at his shirt to take it off him in blatant hunger to have sex with him.

Poppy had done nothing.

Nothing.

This was Poppy back in her observation mode.

He wasn't angry. But he did need to be distracted. He perused the love letter and then strode to his desk, intending to unlock the drawer in which he'd hidden the blackmail letter.

Poppy cleared her throat.

He glanced up.

"Thank you, Nathaniel. That was quite nice."

He could never be angry with Poppy. "How do you feel?"

Her smile was dazzling. "Very pleasantly askew."

He arched an eyebrow as he set the letter back on his desk for a moment and came around to help her put her gown back in order. He wasn't certain what to do about her magnificent cascade of hair, so he merely gathered the pins and held them out to her while she attempted to put it back into fashionable style.

She twirled the long strands so they sat loosely atop her head and began to secure them with the pins.

He watched.

She blushed when she realized he was studying her. "I was quite swept away by your first kiss, too. I don't want you to believe I wasn't. But I felt *you* weren't. I didn't want you to simply indulge me. I wanted it to be special for you, too."

He gave her cheek a light caress. "It was, Poppy. Every kiss between us will always be special and have meaning."

"Because we're friends?"

He nodded. "More than that. We know each other. We have a history together. Kissing you isn't merely about the feel of your mouth against mine. It's about every memory we've shared up to this moment. It's about the little girl with the sunny smile and sweet disposition who stole my clothes on a hot summer's day, the only naughty thing she's ever done in her life. It's about the love you showed my aunt and sister, taking care of them while I was off fighting on the Continent hundreds of miles away."

"You know I would do anything for them."

He nodded and picked up the love letter once more to glance at it. He then unlocked the top drawer of his desk and removed the blackmail letter. "That's why Lavinia trusted you with her secret. That's why I'm going to trust you with *this* letter."

She regarded him in confusion. "You received a letter as well?"

He arched an eyebrow and cast her a wry look. "It is no love letter. This one concerns Lavinia. When did she tell you about the baby?"

"The baby? I only learned of it on this visit."

He shook his head and gave a curt nod. "I suppose it doesn't matter how long you've been aware of Lavinia's secret. What you can't possibly know is that someone else has learned of it and is now threatening to release the scandalous news to the gossip rags. The note you received this morning may have been sent by the same person. I want to compare the handwriting."

She blinked and her face paled. "A blackmail scheme? Why would anyone wish to hurt Lavinia?"

His gaze turned hard as steel. "I don't know. But I mean to destroy the bounder before he can do her any harm. Lavinia cannot know about this. It will break her heart."

She nodded. "I'll help, of course. May I see his letter?"

"Very well, but don't assume it is a man. It could be a female behind this treachery."

Poppy's heart was beating madly as she read it. Had she gotten everything wrong? Nathaniel wasn't the one with the problem. The baby wasn't his but Lavinia's? She strained to think back to their first conversation by the pond. She'd mentioned Lavinia and babies, but had been thinking of *his* child. *His* mistake with Charlotte. A mistake that had never happened. Which meant he was free to marry whomever he wished.

He was free to marry *her.*

But he'd told Penelope he was going to offer for Charlotte.

Was it true?

No, it can't be. He didn't even know the color of her eyes or recall her scent other than to remark she'd probably arrive smelling of sweating horses.

No man in love spoke like that about his beloved.

Her heart beat faster and the little butterflies in her stomach began to flutter.

She'd wasted precious days having him fall in love with Charlotte. Thank goodness he'd been dense as a donkey and learned nothing in all this time.

But Poppy put her elation aside for the moment, for she had to consider this new and most urgent revelation about Lavinia.

Mother in heaven. Lavinia had a secret baby.

Nathaniel had revealed the secret to her believing she already knew it. Of course, it was safe with her and she would never tell a soul, not even Penelope and Olivia.

"I've gotten nowhere on the investigation," Nathaniel said, his brow furrowing as he stared at the letter. "And I can't put my regular men on it because they're outsiders and will draw too much attention if they start asking questions in town. And what can they ask without giving Lavinia's secret away?"

She had to help him, of course.

"I thought to compare both letters. The one sent to Lavinia earlier and the love letter you received today. Hopefully, that will give us some clues."

"No wonder you fairly leaped across the table to snatch it out of my hands." She wanted to cry tears of joy. Was it possible she had a chance with Nathaniel?

She held her breath as she studied the letters while standing beside him. He now held them side-by-side to compare them. "Oh, Nathaniel. They don't look at all alike."

She could not mask her disappointment. They now had two mysteries to solve. Not that finding out the identity of her secret admirer was so important. It could wait.

In truth, she didn't care if his identity was ever discovered.

She'd just kissed the man of her dreams.

But now that he'd read *The Book of Love* from cover to cover and gained all the wisdom it contained, how could she lure him into loving her?

Was it possible these love 'recipes' would work on him anyway?

She wasn't certain, but she'd come up with a plan with the help of Olivia and Penelope.

Nathaniel simply had to fall under her siren spell.

But how did one go about becoming an irresistible siren in the matter of a day?

Chapter Nine

"It seems logical someone had to know Lavinia's secret back when it happened." Poppy concentrated on the blackmail letter and not the handsome man standing beside her, wreaking havoc on her composure. "Perhaps if we begin our search back then, we'll come up with some answers."

Nathaniel stood deliciously close to her.

They were still in his study. Only a few minutes had passed since he'd shaken her to her toes with not one, but two, perfect kisses.

She felt the graze of his muscled shoulders as he leaned forward while they both pored over the blackmail letter again.

"I thought of that, but who other than my grandfather or my parents would have known? They're no longer around to tell me." He grunted in disgust. "The village elders might know who Lavinia's friends were at the time then or if she ever had a beau. But what am I to ask? Were you aware Lavinia had a baby about two years before I was born?"

Poppy sighed. "The identity of her best friend back then is obvious."

"It is?"

She nodded. "Lavinia grew up at Sherbourne. It stands to reason she was friendly with other girls her age. She and Lady Plimpton are about the same age. They've been friends forever. Isn't it obvious?"

"To you, perhaps," he muttered. "Her rat of a nephew must have somehow gotten his hands on–"

"Nathaniel! Stop accusing Andrew Gordon. You have no proof."

"I have something better than proof. I have good instincts." He set the letter down atop his desk and began to flex his hands, curling them and then relaxing them, then repeating the motion.

"For pity's sake. What do you plan to do? Beat a confession out of him?" She met his frown with one of her own. "You're growling again."

"I am not."

"You're giving me that angry wolf look." The swirls of gray and green in his eyes were quite intense and lethal. He reminded her of a predator on the hunt. "What would prompt Lady Plimpton to reveal Lavinia's secret now? And why to him? It doesn't make sense."

"Obviously, she would have done so inadvertently."

She nibbled her lip in thought. "Forget the Plimptons for the moment. There are others who could have found out the information. An old servant."

"Ours are loyal." He folded his arms across his chest, obviously to mark his indignation.

"All of them?"

He looked severe and massive and immovable. "Yes, every last one of them."

She sighed. "A midwife, perhaps. A physician? Not that they would ever send such a note, but someone might have come across old records. A baptismal record? We could ask Vicar Carstairs for permission to view those."

He grumbled.

"You know I'm right."

"I'm the damn earl here. I don't have to ask for anyone's permission."

She rolled her eyes. "Indeed, your lordship. Just stomp into the vicarage and shout your demands."

He dropped his arms to his sides and cast her a wry grin. "Stop kicking my arse. I'm angry. I'm frustrated. I want to beat the stuffing out of the blackguard who wants to hurt my aunt."

She placed a hand on his arm, ignoring the tingle that shot through her the moment her fingers came to rest on his taut muscle. Up close, he was bigger than she realized. Warrior big and his shoulders were broad. His arms were as hard as iron bands.

She stifled a sigh. "So do I. Let's visit the vicar this afternoon. We can stop by Dr. Carmichael's infirmary afterward and ask to sort through his predecessor's records."

"He'll want a reason."

She tipped her gaze up to his. "You're the earl here. You don't have to give a reason."

He grinned, but it soon faded. "Poppy, how long have you known Lavinia's secret?"

"Do you want the truth or an appeasing lie?"

"The truth. Always." He arched an eyebrow, obviously uncertain where this conversation would take them.

"Very well." Indeed, she never wanted to be anything but honest with him. He would be angry, but so be it. One thing she'd learned from reading *The Book of Love* was that trust was vital in order to form those deeper, lasting connections. If Nathaniel did not trust her, then he would never fall in love with her. No amount of seduction would ever work on him.

Not that it mattered, for how did one go about becoming an irresistible seductress? The two glorious kisses they'd shared had come about because she'd demanded to be kissed, practically begged him to kiss her and he'd done so reluctantly. "I know you think Lavinia shared this secret with me, but she didn't."

He shook his head and frowned. "She let it slip somehow, and you were perceptive enough to figure it out?"

"No." She took a deep breath and continued. "You did."

"What? I let it slip?"

She nodded.

He shook his head again and gave a curt, exasperated laugh. "How is it possible? I never said a word to you about it."

"That's true. Until now."

He appeared even more confused, so she pressed on. "All this time, we have been talking of different problems. It all started the other day by the pond when we were speaking of babies and why a man would abandon his wife and child." She took a deep breath to stem the rising ache in her heart. "I thought you were referring to yourself and Lady Charlotte. I thought she was carrying your child and you now had to marry her."

His mouth dropped open.

Then he shut it and shook his head again. "Poppy, how could you think… no wonder you kept bringing her up."

"Is it so farfetched? Why else would you tell me there could never be anything between us? Why else would you invite her to your home when you don't appear to like her very much? And you came right out and told Penelope you intended to marry Charlotte."

"I only said it to rile her because she wouldn't stop hounding me." His eyes widened in horror. "But you spoke about Lavinia and a child. You had to know."

"I didn't. I was referring to your child and meant to assure you that Lavinia would love your child because it was part of you."

He said nothing for the longest moment. "*Bollocks*. You thought I'd been careless and spread my seed."

"And selected Charlotte as… your fertile vessel? Well, yes."

He groaned and ran a hand through his hair. "Are there any other misunderstandings we ought to clear up?"

"I hope not." She cast him a wry smile.

His expression turned tortured. "Hell and damnation. I'm to blame for letting the secret out. How will I ever make it up to Lavinia?"

Poppy put a hand to her throat and gasped. "You've only told me, and I will take it to my grave. I would never betray your aunt. Nor any of your family. Nathaniel, you know I care deeply for all of you." She'd almost blurted she loved him, but managed to stop herself in time. He probably knew it anyway since Farthingales were not alluring women of mystery. Indeed, Farthingale women were meddlesome, always spoke their mind, and managed to get into embarrassing scrapes as easily as they drew their next breath. "Stop blaming yourself. We have a blackmailer to catch."

"We?"

"Yes, we're going to solve this mystery together. Everyone believes we're working through *The Book of Love*. It's the perfect cover for our true intention. So, while everyone believes we are learning about love, you and I will really be spending time tracking down the fiend who means to hurt Lavinia."

He appeared to accept the idea. However, his brow remained furrowed. "What about your mysterious suitor?"

She shrugged. "Let's take his love letter with us. Perhaps we'll spot a match to his handwriting while we search through the vicarage records. But he isn't important."

"Why not?"

"Because I will never marry that man."

He held her back when she gathered the book and started to walk out. "Do you know yet who you wish to marry?"

Lord, were all men this dense?

"I need to give it more thought." She slipped under his arm and waited for him to release his hold on the door. "I'll grab my shawl before we walk to the vicarage. Won't be a moment."

He took a step back, allowing her to open it. "Promise me it won't be that bounder."

"Andrew Gordon? You needn't worry. It isn't."

WATCHING POPPY MOVE was like watching a majestic wave ripple across the water. *Smooth. Graceful. Fascinating.* She had a magnificent wiggle as she hurried upstairs to put away her book and fetch her shawl.

He shouldn't have asked her the question since he already knew the answer.

She wished to marry him.

Yes, she wished for a sacred union while he wished to bed her. She was in love. He was in lust.

It wasn't at all the same thing.

Perhaps if she admitted her love for him, he might dig deep and allow himself to follow his heart. But his heart needed to mend first. He shook his head. He was being an arrogant ass. He was a coward. He knew a girl like Poppy would heal his heart.

Yet, he needed to hear her say it. *I love you, Nathaniel.*

He didn't know why it was so important to have her say those words to him, especially since he wasn't certain how he would respond.

He was only supposed to be her test frog.

He didn't want to feel anything beyond casual friendship. No hurt. No ache. No heart torn to ribbons.

He'd grown used to feeling numb. Numbness was easy. He was comfortable with it.

But Poppy, she turned the heat up inside of him. She made him want things like happiness, children, and hope for the future.

Hell, if he ever gave his heart free rein, he would love her so deeply and whole-heartedly, it scared the life out of him.

Breeding heirs with her would also be so delightful as to be sinful.

He almost groaned aloud, thinking of Poppy and their nights of sex.

But marriage was comprised of more than a few nights of decadent pleasure to create the necessary offspring. Of course, since his brain immediately shut down at the thought of Poppy in his bed, he couldn't list what else mattered in a marriage.

But bedding her was never going to happen outside of wedded bliss.

Not with Poppy.

He glanced up as she hurried back downstairs. "Do you have both letters?" she whispered, casting him a conspiratorial glance.

He leaned close, his lips lightly pressed against her ear and said in a hushed rumble, "I do."

He drew back, ignoring the urge to nibble her ear and nuzzle the slender curve of her neck. "Let's go." He led her out to the garden, toward the rear gate, and to the road that was the shortcut into Wellesford.

"Shall we call on Dr. Carmichael first? Or Vicar Carstairs?"

"Vicarage first," Nathaniel said, hoping Thad hadn't been too rough on the vicar when questioning him about Poppy's love letter. Now they would appear on his doorstep not an hour later demanding more answers. It couldn't be helped. He and Poppy only had a few days to find out who was behind this blackmail threat.

That he'd been the one to spill the secret to Poppy still had his stomach twisted in knots. How could he have been so reckless? Fortunately, he'd made the mistake with her and not someone with a malicious heart.

Poppy was a beautiful girl, but the thing he liked most about her was the genuine goodness of her heart. At times, she was too sweet. But she was still young and uncertain of herself. She had always been shy and reserved.

Perhaps he'd always felt protective of her because of this.

Indeed, she was someone special. Any other young lady would have used Lavinia's secret to her own advantage, perhaps force him into marriage in order to keep the secret quiet. The dastardly thought had never crossed Poppy's mind.

She didn't have a malicious bone in her body.

Thad was just leaving the vicarage when Nathaniel and Poppy appeared. "What are you two doing here? Making certain I haven't killed your precious vicar?"

Nathaniel arched an eyebrow. "Have you?"

Thad grinned. "He's still standing. Why are you here?"

"I wanted to check on some family records," Poppy replied, sparing Nathaniel the need to fabricate a story.

"Farthingales?" Thad nodded. "I didn't know your family had ties to Wellesford."

"Farthingales have ties everywhere." Poppy shook her head and smiled impishly. "We have been likened to a plague of locusts. Although I think it is rather a harsh description. We're a big, loving family. And we're close knit despite being spread out across England."

Thad glanced at Nathaniel and shrugged. "Enjoy. I'll be off now. Your sister has enlisted me to help with your party. She won't have me as her test frog, but is more than willing to use me as her beast of burden."

"We have servants to assist her, Thad. You–"

"I don't mind. Loopy may be irritating at times, but she's never dull." He strode off toward the center of town, hopping the low, stone wall surrounding the vicarage instead of following the graveled path lined with medieval roses that led onto the main road into the village.

The Wellesford vicarage stood on the outskirts of town. One had to pass it when walking from Sherbourne Manor into Wellesford. But it was situated a little back from the road, a sturdy, stone structure situated atop a small hill so that its steeple could be seen from anywhere in the vicinity.

The vicar emerged from his office just as they entered the vicarage. "Lord Welles?" he remarked with some surprise, obviously not expecting his visit. The man fairly tripped over his own two feet to rush forward and greet Poppy. "Miss Farthingale, it is a delight to see you."

"Thank you, Mr. Carstairs. I was hoping you might do me a favor." It took only a smile and a bat of her eyelashes, long, dark lashes that reminded Nathaniel of those of a fawn, to ensorcel this man of the church.

"Anything for you, Miss Farthingale."

She blushed. "Yes, well… I was hoping to have a look at your old baptismal records."

"Certainly. How far back do you wish to search? Our records go back about five hundred years. However, those old records are extremely fragile. I ought to assist you with–"

"It isn't necessary," Nathaniel said, his tone purposely dismissive. "I'm here to help Miss Farthingale. We'll start with the records over the last fifty years and slowly work our way back."

The vicar cast him a wry grin. "Of course, my lord."

"And I'd also like to see Walter Fitch's baptismal record," Poppy said. "Dr. Carmichael mentioned that he was named after me. It's silly really. I'm sure he was in jest, but I'd like to see for myself."

"I'll set you up in my library and bring all those ledgers to you. I only need Walter's ledger back immediately since it is still in current use. But take as much time as you like with the others."

Although the vicar promptly brought the ledgers to the library, to Nathaniel's annoyance, the man took far too long to leave. He found any excuse imaginable to hover close to Poppy. "Thank you, Vicar. We'll call you when we need you," he finally said, for the man had no intention of leaving them otherwise.

Nathaniel waited for the door to close before turning to Poppy. "Thought we'd never be rid of him."

"He was only being polite, Nathaniel. Why were you so rude to him?"

"I wasn't rude. He understood my meaning."

She settled into a chair beside a pile of musty ledgers. "And what was your meaning other than being rude?"

He settled beside her. "I was warning him to keep his hands off you. He may be a man of the church, but his thoughts about you are anything but saintly."

"He was only being polite." She opened the newest ledger and began to peruse it.

"He was lusting after you. Wasn't it obvious?" He took out the two letters. "Let's see if he's the bounder who sent you this love letter. Then we'll get down to the nastier business concerning Lavinia."

They could have looked at any of the entries, but Poppy turned the pages to Walter Fitch's baptismal record first. "Well, the vicar isn't my secret admirer. That's for certain. The handwriting isn't even close. But look, Dr. Carmichael wasn't joking. Walter's full name is Walter Poppy Fitch." She turned to Nathaniel with a starry smile and a look of innocent wonder. "They really did name him after me."

"Are you surprised? You probably saved Mrs. Fitch's life."

She shook her head. "Hardly that. She's a sturdy woman. I had little to do other than hold her hand and calm her down."

Nathaniel caressed her cheek. "The touch of Poppy," he murmured. "Never underestimate its gentle power."

She blushed. "Anyone could have helped her."

"But only you did." Nathaniel knew she didn't take compliments easily, and that made him all the more determined to give her as many as she deserved. Indeed, he needed to make up for all the years he'd ignored her.

Gad, he'd been such a fool.

"Let's start back about thirty years and search forward from there," he said. "Hopefully, something useful will leap out at us."

It didn't take long before Poppy inhaled lightly. "Look, Nathaniel."

He moved closer. "What did you find?"

"I didn't know Miss Billings was born in Wellesford. I thought she'd only moved here a few years ago."

She was referring to the bookshop owner, Felicity Billings. Nathaniel knew his sister liked her and that was saying something, for Penelope took time to warm up to people. Yet, she'd felt comfortable with Miss Billings from their very first encounter. "That's interesting. Let's look closer. *Hell.*"

"What is it? You have such an odd look on your face."

"My grandfather signed as a witness."

Poppy's eyes widened in surprise. "You don't think…"

"What other explanation can there be? Why would my grandfather be at her baptism otherwise? Serving as witness?"

Poppy pursed her lips in thought. "It's so odd. I don't see any resemblance between Lavinia and Miss Billings."

Nathaniel didn't either, but that signified little. "She might take after the father's side of the family."

"I suppose." Poppy began to nibble her lip, the gesture momentarily distracting Nathaniel as he thought of the pleasure he'd have in tasting her lips again.

Bollocks.

He shifted uncomfortably, suddenly aware of the intimacy of their surroundings. The vicarage library was a tiny room filled with old books. The table was small, and they'd had to draw their chairs quite close to each other in order to both fit.

Sunlight filtered in through one small window. Dust motes were dancing amid the lone ray of light. The room smelled dank and musty after the recent rain. But Poppy's scent, that touch of lavender, gave the room a feel of heaven. "We ought to pay a call on her next."

He rose, for another moment beside Poppy and she'd be on his lap, and he'd be kissing her. And doing whatever else his depraved mind wished him to do to the girl.

"Do you mean for us to leave now?" She gazed up at him, confused. "But we've just started. Perhaps your grandfather, or even your father, signed as witness elsewhere. Shouldn't we satisfy that possibility before taking off to accuse poor Miss Billings?"

"Poor Miss Billings?" He frowned at Poppy, not that any of this mess or the turmoil he was feeling at the moment was her fault. "She might be the one attempting to extort payment from her own mother."

Poppy pursed her lips. "That is the act of an angry, bitter person. Miss Billings does not strike me as possessing any of those sentiments. She's very nice and always cheerful."

Nathaniel folded his arms over his chest. "And all the while, she could be plotting her revenge."

"Sit down, Nathaniel. Why don't you take me to town after we've finished perusing these records? You can buy me a lemonade and then we'll pay a call on Miss Billings." She cast him one of her rare, impish smiles. "She has some naughty books that Penelope, Olivia, and I are eager to read."

He groaned. "Naughty books?"

He ought to have been angry, but Poppy never misbehaved except for that one time she'd taken his clothes from the bank of the pond. She'd been casting him impish smirks more often lately, and he liked that she seemed to be coming into her own, no longer feeling she had to be perfect and dutiful.

He was glad she was ready to step into the world and experience some of it, but he didn't want her to experience too much of it. She was still innocent and not to be trusted on her own.

That *he* was the biggest danger to her respectability was of no moment. He'd always do right by Poppy. He had to keep reminding himself of it. If ever they… if ever he… but he wouldn't. And if he did, he'd marry her.

Lord! He'd used the 'M' word. The 'M' signifying peril to all bachelors. Danger. Warning. Sailing into uncharted seas.

"Well, Olivia is going to purchase these books since she's now a married lady and knows about such things. We won't get to read them unless she decides it is safe for us to do so."

He rolled his eyes. "Olivia? An eighteen-year-old girl who has been married merely a week?"

"She is wise beyond her years."

Nathaniel gave a laughing groan and sank back into the chair beside her. "Very well. Let's go through the rest of these entries and see what else turns up."

They scanned the pages through a period of five years and then broadened the search to ten years. Miss Billings remained their best and only lead. They'd also compared Poppy's love letter to every signature and found nothing helpful.

Finally, Poppy arched her back and sighed. "I really thought we'd find something of interest, but there's nothing else here."

He took her hand and helped her to her feet. "I owe you a lemonade. We'll talk about what we've found once we are out of earshot."

They bid Vicar Carstairs farewell.

Nathaniel remained silent as Carstairs spent too long over Poppy's outstretched hand. Lord, he was a fawning dolt. Otherwise, he liked the man.

Would he be as much of a fool when he fell in love?

It wasn't far to the center of town, but Poppy began to use her five senses again as they approached the magistrate's house. She closed her eyes and twirled in a slow circle. "Just feel this beautiful day, Nathaniel."

"Stop dancing about, Poppy. Aren't you thirsty?" He knew he was being surly, but he was not going to explore his feelings just now. He already knew what he was feeling. Anger for the revenge Miss Billings was plotting. Inexplicable lust for Poppy.

Indeed, inexplicable since she had yet to try a single test on him.

And that irritated him to no end.

"I can feel the warmth of the sun as it *touches* my skin."

"Walk in the shade, Poppy. I don't want your skin to burn." *Unless it burns in response to my touch.*

And those errant thoughts were exactly why he had to stop *feeling.*

That damn book.

"*Look* at the birds. How lovely they appear soaring against the blue sky. *Listen* to how happy they sound. They're all chirping at once. Oh, and do you *smell* the aroma of cinnamon buns coming from the bake shop? Are you going to *taste* one, Nathaniel?"

"Poppy, you are as subtle as a battle axe. I will not be manipulated by you or *The Book of Love.*" But he caught her hand and tucked it in the crook of his arm. "Those cinnamon buns smell awfully good. Let's stop there first. We can eat them while you have your lemonade."

"I'd rather have a slice of lemon seed cake. Cinnamon buns

and lemonade don't go together very well."

"As you wish." But afterward, they were going to have a serious discussion with Miss Billings.

Was she Lavinia's blackmailer?

Chapter Ten

"Nathaniel, I think you ought to wait outside while I go in and have a chat with Miss Billings. She'll speak more freely to me while we are alone. Does that plan suit you?"

"Yes." He gave a curt nod. "I intimidate most people. You have a way of making them feel comfortable enough to spill their guts to you."

"Oh, that sounds jolly," she teased.

"Well, you have a gentle manner about you. Anyone would let down their guard and reveal their innermost secrets to you. I certainly did," he muttered, still kicking himself for his lapse in showing her the blackmail letter.

"I won't be long." Poppy took a deep breath and then entered the bookshop. "Good day, Miss Billings."

The chestnut-haired woman with cheerful green eyes came forward to greet her with a smile. "Good day, Miss Farthingale. I'm so glad you stopped by. I just received a shipment of books you and your friends might like. May I show them to you?"

"Of course." Poppy returned her smile and followed her past the rows of shelves into a small room closed off from the shop by a simple green curtain. The room was stacked with boxes, most of them empty. But there were a few that still contained books.

"These came from London only this morning," Miss Billings said in a whisper, as though sharing a secret.

Poppy intended to draw more secrets out of her. "Do tell."

She leaned in conspiratorially.

"Well, I believe there is nothing offensive about them. But some men might take issue with my beliefs. Although they are very different stories, at heart, they are each about women rising above their dire circumstances and doing something to change their lives for the better."

"Interesting. Just how do they better their circumstances? By underhanded means?"

Miss Billings took on a faraway expression as she pondered the question. "No, although others might not agree. How is it underhanded when one is pushed to the brink and must do something drastic to save themselves or those they love?"

"Do they hurt others while saving themselves? Then I would have to conclude such means are underhanded."

"Perhaps." She cast Poppy a wistful look. "Not everyone is fortunate to have a loving family or good friends to turn to when in need of rescue. Many people are quite alone in the world. I believe these stories speak to them."

Poppy gave the woman's hand a light squeeze. "Oh, dear. Miss Billings, how thoughtless of me. I never asked about your family or your circumstances growing up. Let's have a cup of tea and talk. You have friends here in Wellesford. You mustn't ever feel you are on your own. And please, call me Poppy. Friends needn't be formal with each other."

She appeared ready to refuse, but quickly relented and cast her another smile. "Please call me Felicity. It feels rather nice to have a friend. I had a few at the orphanage, of course. But we all went our separate ways."

"I'm so sorry, Felicity. Is that where you grew up? At an orphanage? Was it near Wellesford?" Poppy followed her into another room just behind the display shelves. It turned out to be a small kitchen.

"Yes, the place is only a few towns away from here. The Birdsong Home for Orphaned Girls. I visit there every once in a while, although not as often as I would like. I was not unhappy there. In truth, I was well cared for. But I never knew who my parents were," she said, suddenly blushing and obviously worried that Poppy would think the lesser of her for it. "I would have liked to learn about them. One feels adrift when one doesn't know who they belong to."

She turned away and put the kettle on to boil, then began to fuss unnecessarily while setting out teacups on her table.

Poppy realized the woman was flustered. "Did you ever ask the headmistress at the orphanage about your parents? Surely she would have some idea of your family connections. Someone had to have brought you there and made provisions for your care."

"Oh, I'm sure the headmistress knows. But she won't tell me." She gave a bitter laugh and motioned toward the shop. "My parents were people of means, I think. They left me a trust fund. Not a large one, but enough for me to purchase this shop and still have enough left over to support me, so long as I live modestly."

Poppy's heart went out to her, for her own family was big and loving. She could not imagine being alone in the world. "I have a sister. Her name is Violet. And lots of cousins. We're all named after flowers. My Uncle John and Aunt Sophie have five daughters. Lily, Daffodil, Daisy, Laurel, and Rose. My Uncle George has a son called William." She grinned. "We called him Sweet William when he was younger because we wanted him to be a flower, too."

Felicity laughed. "That sounds wonderful."

"We Farthingales meddle in each other's business. Always with the best of intentions, of course. We'd never do anything to hurt each other."

The kettle began to whistle, and Felicity quickly crossed the room to remove it from the heat and pour the steaming water into their cups. "The holidays must have been lovely for you."

Poppy nodded. "They were. We children played with each other for hours on end and often slept four in a bed because we couldn't bear to be parted even at bedtime."

"That's what I miss most." She wiped a tear and laughed. "I

was given a good education and never lacked for food. I was well clothed and well-tended. I was given kindness, but never shown love. That is what I wished for most when I was young. I dreamed of having that sort of love with my family. I dreamed of *belonging*. But it was not meant to be."

"You mustn't give up on any of it," Poppy said after hurriedly swallowing a sip of her tea. "What if Lord Welles and I were to take you back to the Birdsong Orphanage and demand to see your records? He's a powerful earl. They won't refuse him."

Felicity looked surprised, but not fearful. "Do you think he would? How can I ask him? Why would he care to help me out?"

"Wellesford is his town. He is protective of its citizens. You are not beneath his notice. He isn't pompous like that. In truth, he's quite splendid." Poppy clamped her mouth shut, determined to say no more. In another moment, she'd be confessing how ardently she admired him.

She supposed her face gave it all away, for she hadn't yet learned to hide her feelings.

"You're in love with him," Felicity said quietly. "I don't blame you. He's quite a handsome man. I expect most of the women in this village feel the same as you do, but you're the only one he would ever seriously consider."

Poppy sighed. "He's invited Lady Charlotte Winthrow and her father to join us for the weekend."

"Oh, I see. The duke and his daughter. I hear she's quite beautiful. I'm so sorry, Poppy. Truly, I am."

"Charlotte hasn't won him yet. I'm going to fight for him." She glanced up, startled at herself for deciding to take action. But this was her heart at stake. If she didn't fight for her happiness now, when would she ever?

Felicity gave a little cheer. "Hurrah! I shall pray very hard for your success."

"Thank you. And I shall speak to Lord Welles about your orphanage. Can you close your shop for the day? We could go there tomorrow."

"Oh, dear. It isn't possible. I've started a reading club and we meet tomorrow at midday. I'll never be through in time. And I hate to cancel it when we've just started meeting. It's new, and I'm afraid it will all fall apart if I'm not here to keep it going." She sighed. "I've waited this long to find out who I am. I can wait a few more days."

Poppy finished her tea and rose. "Then we'll plan it for another day. I won't forget, and I promise you, I'll speak to Lord Welles about your situation." After choosing a rather saucy book about a spinster's adventures in Italy with a mysterious count who awakened her to the joys of womanhood, she left to find Nathaniel.

She found him seated alone in a quiet corner of the Golden Hart, a pint of ale before him. He rose eagerly the moment she entered the establishment. "How did it go?"

He glanced down at her book, noted the title, and groaned. "*Lady Cordelia's Tuscan Adventure*? Just what sort of adventure does she have?"

"A love adventure, of course. She's an innocent English rose that the count has plucked from his garden. You see, she's on a tour of his majestic home and he sees her standing in his garden amid a bed of roses. Ergo, he plucks her out of–"

"Is that what they call the act of ruining a young lady?"

"She isn't ruined. It's romantic."

"Being *plucked* is not romantic. Does he marry her after he ruins her?"

She frowned at him. "I don't know. I haven't read it yet. I'll let you know the outcome once I finish it."

He shook his head and settled beside her when she took her chair. But he leaned close and was frowning back at her. *Goodness, he has the most gorgeous eyes.* "I don't care about Lady Cordelia's misadventures," he said. "Obviously, we are talking about you. Couldn't you have chosen something more suitable to read?"

"Something boring, you mean? No. It's only a book, Nathaniel. I am not about to let myself be *plucked* by just any man."

"Lord help me," he muttered, rolling his eyes. "Banish that word from your vocabulary. What of Miss Billings? Did you find out anything useful about her background?"

She nodded. "Clear your schedule for tomorrow."

"Why?"

"We are going to the Birdsong Home for Orphaned Girls. That's where Felicity was raised. I mean, Miss Billings. Well, we are on first-name terms now. We are friends."

He cast her a wry smile. "That didn't take long."

"I truly like her. I hope she isn't the villain." Poppy shook her head and continued her report. "She never knew her parents, but someone established a trust fund for her. She purchased the bookshop with those funds. More important, payments must have been sent regularly to the orphanage by someone of means. Felicity was educated and well cared for while growing up."

"And you suspect it was my grandfather who made those payments? Probably my father who continued them after my grandfather passed."

"I think it's likely. Don't you?"

He sighed. "Yes."

"Oh, and I looked at the handwriting in her ledger while she was distracted by another customer. It is nothing like either of those letters. I don't think she's the culprit. But I think we ought to look closely at the headmistress of the Birdsong Orphanage."

"I'll ride there in the morning."

"You? Alone?" Poppy could not mask her disappointment. "Without me?"

"I would very much like to take you with me, but how can I without bringing along a chaperone for you? Our traveling together would require this, and I dare not bring someone else in on the secret. Besides, I'll travel faster on my own."

He was right, she supposed. "Very well."

He caressed her cheek when she gazed down in disappointment. "I wish I could bring you with me, Poppy. You'd crack this mystery wide open within minutes of meeting the headmistress.

I'll do my clumsy best without you."

"I expect you'll do just fine without me. May I make up a list of questions for you?"

He arched an eyebrow and cast her a tender smile. "I don't do well with lists. Just tell me what you think I ought to ask. Also, I'd rather not have anything in writing about this delicate subject."

"Oh, I see. You're right."

He downed the last of his ale and took her hand to help her up. "Thank you, Poppy. I want you to know how much I appreciate all you're doing for Lavinia. Most of all, it eases my mind to know you're not judging her. It gives me hope that others won't either, especially her dearest friends. But people can be cruel. I'm not sure she'll come out of this scandal with her heart intact."

They walked back to Sherbourne Manor together. Poppy's mind was awhirl with questions to ask. "First, find out if the headmistress is new or has been in charge all these years."

"And if she's new?"

Poppy pursed her lips. "Don't trust her."

"And if she's the old headmistress?"

"Don't trust her."

He grinned. "Duly noted. It's all right, Poppy. I know what to ask. My only concern is that I will not get the answers I need. My manner often frightens and intimidates. People close up around me. They're respectful, but they won't ever confide in me. You'd get them to open up and pour out their secrets. People genuinely like you. They'll think nothing of opening their hearts to you."

He paused a moment, obviously contemplating whether to reconsider his decision not to take her along. "I think you could get anyone at the orphanage to open up to you," he said softly and with a touch of awe. "The laundress, the groundskeeper. Even the orphans."

"Then, may I go?" She tried not to sound too hopeful.

"No. I do wish to take you with me, but it can't be done. Perhaps next time, assuming another visit is required."

She nodded. "I'd like that."

Beast and Goose were in the parlor with Lavinia, Penelope, and Thad when they returned to the manor. Penelope and Goose cast her hopeful, quizzical glances.

She shook her head slightly to convey they ought not get their hopes up. She knew Nathaniel had enjoyed her company, but it did not signify anything.

However, he seemed to be studying her throughout supper. And studying her after supper when they all walked into the music room to hear Olivia play the pianoforte. Was he hoping to get her alone to ask more questions?

She sidled over to him when the others moved closer to the pianoforte to sing along to Olivia's music. "What else do you wish to know?" she asked him once they were both standing beside the doors leading onto the terrace and could speak softly without being overheard.

"Nothing."

"Nothing?" She tipped her head up and frowned in confusion. "Then why were you staring at me all evening long?"

He shoved his hands in his pockets and leaned his big shoulder against one of terrace doors. "Was I? I hadn't noticed."

"You know you were. If it wasn't to catch my attention to ask me more questions, then why?"

He shrugged. "There's something different about you tonight." He eyed her up and down. "But I can't figure out what you've done to yourself. So, I give up. Your trick worked. Tell me what changed."

"My trick?" She hadn't done anything yet. Although she intended to set up a plan of action with Olivia and Penelope tomorrow while Nathaniel was away. She wanted to be prepared for Charlotte's visit. She was determined to thwart the Incomparable's design on Nathaniel.

"Is it your hair? You've done it up differently."

She stifled a grin. Was it possible he was looking at her for the first time as a desirable woman? Really looking at her and liking what he saw. "No, it's the same style as always."

He leaned close and inhaled lightly along her neck, causing tingles to shoot through her body. "Your scent?"

She arched an eyebrow and chuckled. "Are you thinking of cinnamon buns again?"

He cast her a boyish grin. "Always. But your scent is lavender."

Something sparked in his gaze, causing more tingles. Could this be happening? He'd read *The Book of Love* and understood how women enticed men. She hadn't done anything differently to lure him. She was herself. *He* was the one who'd changed. More precisely, he had stopped thinking of her as his sister's best friend and was now considering her as a desirable female.

This was so exciting!

She couldn't wait to report her findings to Olivia and Penelope.

Take that Lady Charlotte!

Indeed, this was monumental. A major shift in the way Nathaniel regarded her.

It felt nice to be seen as a woman in his eyes, and a tempting one at that.

She had never been a temptress before.

It was a heady, enjoyable feeling.

Nathaniel quirked his eyebrow. "Now you're staring at me. Why?"

She couldn't help it. In this respect, men and women were similar. Each made instinctive assessments of the qualities they wished for in a suitable mate. Since women needed men to love and protect not only them but also their offspring, women looked for more than a beautiful body. They looked for strength and power. They wanted a man with muscles and intelligence.

Warrior strong.

Able to fight off wolves.

Nathaniel was that man for her, but how was she to firm the bond between them when he was riding to the orphanage tomorrow, and Charlotte would arrive the day after that? "I'm doing no such thing. Excuse me a moment, Nathaniel. I think your sister is calling me over."

She darted to Penelope's side. "I need your help," she whispered in her ear, distracting her from Olivia's recital. "It's about your brother."

Penelope's eyes widened and she grinned. "Come with me." She grabbed Poppy's hand and hustled her out of the music room. "What sort of help do you need? I'll do anything to keep him out of the clutches of Lady Charlotte."

Poppy did not need her friend to take drastic action. After all, Nathaniel had to fall in love with her of his own free will. How else would they ever have a happy marriage? "Your brother was staring at me throughout the evening."

Penelope gasped. "He was?"

Poppy nodded. "I must have been doing something to tempt him. I just don't know what it was. Is there something different about me tonight?"

Penelope took a step back to study her. "Well, you're very pretty."

"Oh, thank you. But is it in a different way than I was before? Have I changed?"

"No. Not that I can tell." She pursed her lips and frowned. "Even your gown is modest. No hint of..." Suddenly, her features lightened and she grinned. "Oh, my goodness. It's your necklace."

Poppy stared down at her chest. "What about my necklace?"

"Do you see that it disappears into your bodice?"

She was about to draw it out when Penelope stopped her. "Good grief, I never thought my brother was as dense as every other male in existence. Don't you see? Your necklace drew his eyes to your breasts. The valley between them, to be precise. Oh, this is rich! He behaved just as the book predicted. The moment his eyes were drawn *there,* his low brain took over. *Healthy breasts. Want that female.*"

"But my gown is modest. How can he see anything of–"

"That's the beauty of it. He can't actually see what lies hidden beneath the fabric, so his low brain is filling in what it wants to see. This is incredible. Olivia had to take drastic action to make Beast notice her, but you didn't need to do a thing." She placed her hands on Poppy's shoulders. "I'm so proud of you. You have ensorcelled my brother. He's falling in love with you and he doesn't even realize it."

Poppy didn't have the heart to disagree with Penelope. Perhaps Nathaniel had fallen in lust with her for the evening, but he was still a long way from loving her. This was Penelope filling in what she herself desired, to have her marry Nathaniel and make them truly be sisters.

The music stopped. In the next moment, Olivia rushed out. "What did I miss?"

Penelope quickly filled her in on their discussion.

Olivia grinned from ear to ear. "I hear Nathaniel has been called away on business tomorrow. We're going to use the time to work on you, Poppy. When he returns, he's going to take one look at you and his heart will slam like a cannonball into his chest."

Poppy did not like the idea of all eyes on her and Nathaniel, but she'd brought her friends into this and they were not going to back off now. "Isn't his heart already in his chest?"

Penelope rolled her eyes. "Yes, but the point is to get it beating wildly out of control. To turn him into a mindless, low brain, unthinking male who will now connect you with pleasurable sex."

Goose nodded. "Poppy. Sex. And the more he thinks it and repeats it, the deeper it embeds in his low-functioning brain."

"Penelope! Goose!" Nathaniel punctuated each name with a beastly growl.

The two of them gasped and then laughingly ran back into the music room. Poppy was left alone with Nathaniel. "You heard?"

She took a hesitant step back as he came toward her. But

she'd been standing close to the hallway wall and there was nowhere else to go. Nathaniel planted his hands on either side of her to trap her against the wall. "Unthinking male. Pleasurable sex. Yes, I heard all of it."

Poppy swallowed hard. "Your sister got a little carried away. You know she wants us to be a match. I think she wants it more than either of us do."

He nodded.

His eyes were as hot and dark as smoldering embers. Emerald embers.

She cleared her throat. "Nathaniel, if you're not going to kiss me, would you mind moving away?"

Whatever passion he'd felt toward her quickly extinguished. Those hot, dark eyes of his filled with anger. He stepped away, dropping his hands to his sides. "Come with me, Poppy."

She hesitated. "I don't think I want to."

He sighed and gave a wry laugh. "No, why would you? I'm merely your test frog. You wanted me to jump and I jumped. Now the test is over. I behaved just as you wished me to behave. You're happy. My sister is dementedly happy." He glanced toward the music room. "Even my own friends are cheering you on."

Poppy groaned.

"Don't ever manipulate me again. No tricks. No magical recipes from *The Book of Love*. Promise me."

She nodded. "I promise."

He eased his taut body and cast her an exasperated but endearing smile. "Good," he said, caressing her cheek.

"Nathaniel, there's just one thing."

"What is it?"

She took a deep breath and then let it out slowly, for his nearness was filling her senses and she ached for him to kiss her. "I wasn't testing you."

He stared at her in confusion.

"There was no test. I wasn't making you jump. I don't even

know what made you jump. Your sister had her suspicions. I'd be ever so grateful if you told me what I did."

"You don't know?" His look of confusion turned to one of utter horror. "Blessed saints! You don't know."

"Was it my necklace? The way it dangled between…" She did not bother to finish her sentence, for his gaze immediately shot to her chest again.

"Blessed saints," he said in a hoarse whisper and strode out the front door, closing it with a slam.

Chapter Eleven

Nathaniel. Test frog. Day four.
We are at a tipping point.

NATHANIEL RODE OFF to the Birdsong Orphanage shortly after sunrise, eager to be away from Sherbourne Manor and all those prying eyes. He rode into the mist, for the sun had yet to burn away the tendrils of gray that hovered over the meadow and hid the pond from view. Even the majestic entry gate was engulfed in its shroud.

Lord, what was he to do about Poppy?

He'd purposely left early to avoid seeing her. Was it true? She'd done nothing but be herself last night? If it were so, and nothing had changed in her, then something must have changed in him.

"Bollocks." He'd read *The Book of Love* and understood what his response represented. The bonds between him and Poppy were deepening. She'd passed his low-brain 'this is a fertile female' test. She'd also passed his 'this is a desirable female and I want to spill my seed into her vessel' test. But to suddenly become the *only* female he wanted?

When did that happen? To go from feeling nothing… well, never nothing. He'd always liked her, but in a friendly way. Then he'd wanted to kiss her.

Then he'd wanted to kiss only her.

And now he wanted only her to warm his bed. Every night

for the rest of their lives?

If this was so, what was he to do about it?

He had also wanted Charlotte Winthrow.

He'd *taken* Charlotte. If anything, the bonds of commitment should have been stronger between them, but they weren't. That *taking* had only been about sex. Perhaps, had Charlotte's heart been involved, it would have meant something more. But it hadn't been. At least, he didn't think so, and his instincts rarely proved wrong.

Nor did he believe he was anyone special to Charlotte. There had been no promises exchanged. No confessions of undying love. He wasn't her first, and the contractual assurances negotiated in any betrothal contract entered into with her father would have included a requirement of her fidelity to ensure the offspring were his.

He grunted in disgust. How could he ever consider such a thing? It was a standard condition in such contracts, but to contemplate marriage to a woman he knew would carry on affairs with other men as soon as she'd given him the necessary male heirs?

He shook out of the thought and concentrated on his purpose in riding to the orphanage. He'd find out all he could about Felicity Billings and her benefactor. He'd discuss his findings with Poppy, try to avoid being swallowed up in the beautiful blue of her eyes, and then they'd both have a talk with Lavinia.

He had wanted to spare his aunt, but Poppy was right. He could not hide the truth from her any longer. She had to be prepared to defend herself if he could not stop the blackmailer.

The headmistress, a tiny, gray-haired whirlwind by the name of Miss Huskins-Eeling, greeted him by the orphanage stables with an open smile. She did not appear to be at all devious or wary. The girls working in the stables greeted them cheerfully, obviously not afraid of this twittering, bird-like woman who seemed capable of handling ten things at once.

"What brings you here, Lord Welles?" she asked, motioning

toward the orphanage, a surprisingly quaint, but big and rambling manor house that appeared in need of some repair. However, for the most part, it appeared sound, having a solid foundation and good bones.

She nodded to every girl they passed in the courtyard as she led him to her office and all returned her acknowledgment with a smile.

If this woman was corrupt, she certainly hid it well.

"I gave your man all the information he requested," she said, casting him a light frown as they entered the orphanage and made their way down the hall. He noted the place smelled clean and the aroma emanating from the kitchen was of a hearty stew. "I told him in no uncertain terms I was not authorized to reveal more to him. Why is Miss Billings so important to you that you should come here yourself?"

Nathaniel frowned. "You think I sent a man to you? When? And what did you tell him?"

She stopped in her tracks and regarded him with astonishment. "Are you suggesting you sent no one here to inquire about Felicity Billings?"

"It is no mere suggestion. I am stating it as fact. Someone is using Miss Billings as a means to do harm to others of my acquaintance. I need to put an end to this mischief before more damage is done."

Her eyes rounded in alarm. "Felicity is a sweet, lovely girl. I hope you don't think she has anything to do with whatever nasty business is afoot."

She hustled him into her office and shut the heavy, wooden door behind them. "Do sit down, my lord. I think we have much of importance to discuss."

It took a mere half hour for Nathaniel to learn all he needed to know. He remained another hour to tour the grounds and discover all he could about this remarkable place and the extraordinary woman who ran it. Although Miss Huskins-Eeling appeared indestructible, not even she would live forever. What would happen to this orphanage and the girls under her care if she was not around to protect them?

He rode off with his thoughts in turmoil.

By the description she had given him of the man who'd come around asking questions about Miss Billings, Nathaniel had a good idea who was behind this blackmail plot. However, the information Miss Huskins-Eeling had given the man would have led him to the wrong conclusion.

The blackmailer, who could be none other than Andrew Gordon, had focused his malice on the wrong target.

Nathaniel was determined to stop him before he caused more harm.

Among the many thoughts swirling in his head was one of Poppy. She would be proud of how quickly he'd gotten to the truth. He couldn't wait to tell her what he'd found out. Yes, it troubled him that she was becoming so important to him and that he looked forward to confiding in her.

But he trusted her, and was eager to discuss his findings with her.

He was also curious to see her response. He wasn't looking for compliments or flattery, but wanted confirmation he had not overlooked something important. Poppy understood people far better than he ever would.

Perhaps riding under the heat of the midday sun was not the brightest idea, but his horse had been well tended to while in the orphanage stables and easily made the journey home at a fast clip.

Nathaniel reached Sherbourne Manor around three o'clock in the afternoon.

Quickly dismounting, he handed the reins to his groom and strode into the house in search of Poppy. "Soames, have you seen Miss Farthingale?"

Perhaps he ought to have been more discreet, but he no longer cared. Everyone adored Poppy down to the last member of his staff. He was fighting a losing battle and he knew it. When he looked at her, he no longer saw just a pretty girl, but a beautiful woman. When he spoke to her, he no longer viewed her as quiet and dull, but thoughtful and intelligent. She was shy, but he liked that she always felt comfortable around him so she could be herself.

She didn't blow through the house like a gale-force wind as his sister was prone to do. No, Poppy was a gentle summer breeze that he always found refreshing. Perhaps that explained why the kisses they'd shared were not just kisses, but came laden with a host of good memories that lightened his heart.

"She's in the garden, my lord. Having tea with–"

"Thank you, Soames." He strode outdoors and looked for her beside one of the large shade trees where the ladies often enjoyed afternoon tea in the summers. It took him a moment to spot her, for she was seated alone on a bench and appeared to be talking to herself.

He grinned.

Indeed, he was truly lost if he thought talking to oneself was charming.

Then he realized she was not alone and had actually been speaking to someone. Smiling at that someone.

Bollocks.

She was with that villain, Andrew Gordon.

His blood immediately heated to a boil. He'd never been this enraged, not even in the midst of battle. Soldiers who fought and killed on either side did it for love of their country and duty to their monarch. But this slimy toad was purposely destroying innocent lives to further his own unscrupulous interests. "Bastard," he said in a low growl, grabbing the man and hauling him up by his lapels.

Gordon let out a yelp and began to swing at him.

Nathaniel knocked him to the ground with a single, well-placed punch.

"Nathaniel, are you mad? What have you done?" Poppy was now on her feet and blazing angry. Her eyes were as wide and tumultuous as a stormy ocean. He'd never seen her this angry.

Indeed, he'd never seen her angry at all. Not ever.

Gordon was moaning and trying to roll to his feet.

Nathaniel used his booted foot to push him back down. "Stay there and don't move," he ordered, ignoring the daggers Poppy was hurling at him with her gaze. "I have business with you, Gordon."

"What sort of business involves beating a man when he's down?" Poppy had her own hands in fists.

"I didn't beat him when he was down. I hit him while he was up. And I'm not letting him up again until I'm done with him. Get out of the way, Poppy. I don't want you hurt."

"While you beat him senseless? I will do no such thing." She tipped her chin up stubbornly, her gaze one of defiance. "I won't allow you to kill him."

"He doesn't deserve your protection." He gave the man another shove when he attempted to get up. "Why were you asking questions about Miss Billings at the orphanage? And pretending to do so at my request?"

Poppy gasped and her fiery gaze shot to Andrew Gordon. "You did that?"

"He's lying," Gordon shot back, rubbing his jaw. "Can't you see he's jealous and trying to destroy my reputation? Don't believe him, Miss Farthingale. What possible reason would I have to be at an orphanage?"

"You tell me, Mr. Gordon." She now had her anger trained on the knave who was sprawled on the ground. "Lord Welles is no liar. Don't waste your breath trying to convince me he is anything other than noble."

"Noble? Hah! That's a good one." He glowered at Nathaniel. "Does she know about you and Lady Charlotte? That you've soiled the Duke of Winthrow's precious daughter. But now you've found Miss Farthingale the more interesting victim and intend to soil her, too. Only she doesn't have a duke for a father to protect her from–"

Nathaniel's control snapped.

He hauled the man to his feet and struck him again.

Gordon fought back, but his fist only managed to graze the side of Nathaniel's head. That was all Nathaniel needed to justify knocking the man down again.

Poppy was yelling for him to stop, but he couldn't. Andrew Gordon intended to make a career out of blackmail. Perhaps he'd already sent notes to Charlotte threatening to reveal her unmaidenly ways to her stern and imposing father.

Poppy's words came back to haunt him. Why do you think she never laughs, Poppy had asked when speaking of Charlotte. Lord, how long had Andrew Gordon been blackmailing her? He wasn't in love with Charlotte, but he was not about to see her destroyed by this vermin.

"Nathaniel, stop! You'll kill him!" Poppy was now tugging on his arm.

Then she was no longer holding him back. Beast and Thad were hauling him off the slimy toad and pinning his arms so he couldn't land another punch. "Let me go!"

His friends ignored him.

Beast turned to Poppy. "What happened?"

"I'm not sure. Nathaniel charged at Captain Gordon like a raging bull." Her voice was shaking as she spoke. Her body was shaking, too.

Damn it, he'd scared her.

Did that mean Poppy believed the cur? How could she? He grunted in frustration and then grunted again when Penelope and Goose rushed to Poppy's side. He frowned at all of them. "The man deserves to die."

Thad kept his arm in a firm grip, his expression warning he'd break it if Nathaniel didn't stop struggling. "Och, be careful what ye wish for. Ye may very well have killed him. I don't think he's conscious. There's blood all over the both of ye. It's on Poppy's gown, too."

He cursed under his breath. "Poppy, I'm sorry. I–"

"Save your apologies for Charlotte. I don't care." She turned and fled into the house.

Penelope kicked him in the shin, then she and Goose hurried after Poppy.

He gazed down at Captain Gordon who was now motionless on the ground.

The fight rushed out of him and he stopped struggling against his friend's grasp. "Thad, let me go." To his relief, his friend did as he asked.

"Shall I summon the magistrate?" Beast asked.

Nathaniel shook his head. "No. Let's revive him. He isn't dead. I can see he's still breathing. I need to speak in private with Lord and Lady Plimpton. They will arrange for him to be shipped off to some far-away posting where he can never hurt anyone again."

Thad nodded. "Assuming he recovers."

Nathaniel spared the knave another glance. "He'll recover. Scheming bastards like him always do."

"Care to tell us what he did?" Beast asked.

"No." Nathaniel glanced down at his bloodied knuckles, withdrew the handkerchief he carried in his breast pocket, and wiped it across the back of his hands. "He's dangerous. Don't trust him. And don't let him near the girls."

"Your nose is bleeding," Thad said, his tone revealing he was aching to hear what was really going on.

Nathaniel knew that neither of his friends would press him on the matter.

This was the difference between men and women. Men did not press each other for information. They merely took in what was offered and gave an appropriate response. Women took in *feelings*. They would not stop asking questions until they'd wrung him dry.

He marched upstairs, leaving a now recovering Gordon in the care of his friends.

On the way up, he ordered his butler to send word to the Plimptons to come to Sherbourne Manor at once. "It is not a request. It is a command. Make certain they understand."

He strode down the hall to his room, but paused when he noticed Poppy's door was open. Goose and Penelope were fussing over her while she dunked a cloth into a basin. She squeezed the water out of it and began to wipe it across her hands. He thought of Lady Macbeth's scene as she was driven mad from the gore of so many murders.

Poppy was no Lady Macbeth, but she was obviously troubled by the way he'd handled matters. Or rather, by the way she felt he'd lost control of matters. "I'd like to speak to Poppy, alone," he said, stopping in her doorway and folding his arms across his chest for no purpose other than he didn't want to reach out and take her into his arms.

She would rebuff him.

She loathed him at the moment.

He wasn't proud of himself, either. But he would not have done anything differently. Andrew Gordon had proved himself to be more dangerous than even he realized. "I'm not giving you a choice. I will speak to Poppy alone whether she wishes it or not. Get out, Penelope. And you, Goose."

They waited for Poppy's nod before walking out.

Nathaniel closed the door behind them.

"You shouldn't be in here, Nathaniel."

"I know. But there's no one here to tattle and ruin you."

She did not look convinced. "And what will you do if word gets out you and I were alone in my bedchamber? Marry me? I don't need you doing me any favors."

Of course, he'd marry her. It didn't require a conversation. He'd never allow any harm, whether physical or mere gossip, to befall Poppy. "I warned you to keep away from that snake." He knew he was pouring oil onto an already kindled fire, but he no longer cared. The sight of Poppy alone with Andrew Gordon still had his stomach twisted in knots.

"I was about to do just that when you came charging down upon us." She wiped the damp cloth along the slender curve of her neck. "I wasn't *entertaining* him. Captain Gordon must have hopped over the stone wall as a shortcut to the manor house. He came upon me as I was reading under the shade tree. He arrived mere moments before you did. Perhaps he'd been there longer and waited for Penelope and Goose to leave. They were out there with me for most of the time. There, you now have my explanation. Not that I owe you one."

She turned away to dunk the cloth into her basin and then began to run it along the curve of her jaw.

"Let me do it," he said in a raw whisper, taking the cloth from her grasp. "You also have a little blood in your hair."

She didn't protest. "Oh, Nathaniel. Why did you do it?"

"He was the one who went to the orphanage looking to expose the secret of Miss Billings' lineage. He forged my calling card. He forged my handwriting in a letter designed to gain access to sensitive records. He probably disguised his handwriting on the letters you and Lavinia received. Who knows what else he's forged and how many other secrets he's found out? I'm sure he asked questions about the other girls at the orphanage while he was there. What better place to dig for secrets but where those of the Upper Class hide their mistakes?"

Poppy's anger seemed to fade as he spoke, and her expression turned thoughtful. "And the headmistress?"

Nathaniel gently dabbed the cloth across her cheek. "She is either the cleverest monster who has ever lived or she's an angel. I think it is the latter. The girls are well cared for. They smile and are not afraid of strangers. She appears to be tirelessly devoted to them."

He also dabbed at Poppy's lips, wishing to bend down and kiss them, but Poppy was still overset. He wasn't that much of an idiot to think he could kiss her into forgiveness when he still had a lot of explaining to do.

He took a deep breath and continued. "I think he's also blackmailing Charlotte."

"What?" She shook her head as though uncertain she'd heard

him correctly. "Because you had relations with her?"

"It could have been with me. I won't deny it. But it was before…" He couldn't very well say it was before he'd met Poppy because he'd known the girl forever and had only started paying close attention to her a few days ago. "I wasn't the first. She wasn't… the point is, I was in a bad way. I…" His voice trailed off again. "I'm not going to marry Charlotte, but neither do I wish to see her hurt. Nor do I wish Lavinia to be hurt. But there's one very important thing you should know."

"And what is that important thing?"

"Lavinia isn't Felicity's mother."

Poppy's mouth gaped open. "Are you certain?"

He nodded. "My grandfather, at Lavinia's tearful urging I expect, stepped forward to protect the child. No doubt, he was also protecting Lavinia's friend who carried the child. You and I need to sit down with her to learn the full story. But I think I've figured out most of it."

He still held the damp cloth in his hand and resumed rubbing it ever so lightly across Poppy's cheek. Lord, he wanted to kiss her so badly.

Her eyes grew wide as saucers. "Your aunt's best friend was Lady Plimpton. Oh, how stupid of me! How did I not notice the resemblance sooner? But why summon Lord Plimpton as well?" She began to nibble her lip and fret. "The secret could destroy their marriage."

"I have no intention of revealing the secret to either of them. All they need to know is he attempted to forge my signature. That ought to be enough to ensure their worthless nephew is sent away. Far away. Banished from England for the rest of his life."

"Do you think Lady Plimpton will know we've found out the truth?"

"I hope not." He ran a hand raggedly through his hair. "I don't wish her to feel scared or humiliated whenever she sees us. If it does come up, I'll leave it to you to assure her the secret is safe with us."

He handed her back the cloth and was about to turn away when Poppy put a hand on his arm. "I'm glad you were able to find all this out before anyone was hurt. Other than her rat of a nephew, of course. How is he?"

"I didn't kill him or permanently maim him. Men such as he always recover." He frowned. "I'll bring the Plimptons into my study and tell them vaguely of his blackmail schemes. I won't mention the orphanage. I won't mention any names. It will be enough to let them know he used my good name for his nefarious purposes."

Poppy's shoulders sagged.

He took her into his arms. "Poppy, I'm sorry. For everything."

She rested her head against his chest and nodded. "So am I. Let's take care of this blackmail matter and then I'm going to move in with Beast and Olivia. Perhaps I'll go home instead. They're still newly married, and I don't want to impose on their privacy. They'll be polite and say they don't mind. But they will. Yes, I think I had better go home."

"Poppy, no. I know I behaved like a raging arse, but surely you understand why."

"I do. And I'm proud of the way you are protecting Lavinia and her dear friend. But I don't think I can do this, Nathaniel. I can't be here when Charlotte, her father, and your Society friends arrive. They won't want me here either."

"They won't stay long. They'll be gone after this weekend. I don't want you to leave."

She squeezed her eyes shut. "I was determined to fight for you. I wanted you to notice me. I wanted you to fall in love with me. But your world is so very different from my own. Yours is one of secrets and elegant facades. Appearances are everything, even to you. Appearances are everything, no matter who is hurt."

"How have I hurt anyone?" He tipped her chin up so her gaze would meet his, but she refused to look him squarely in the eyes. "Surely, you can't be siding with Andrew Gordon."

"Of course not. This isn't about him."

"Yes, it is. It's about him and my determination to pound him into dust. It's about Charlotte and my casual dalliance with her. Look at me, Poppy. How do you think Thad or Beast or I survived the war? By behaving like gentlemen? Out on the battlefield, it is kill or be killed. Protect your own. Trust your friends to watch your back. It is no different when an enemy attempts to destroy you in your own home. I will never allow anyone to hurt my family. I will fight. I will kill to protect those I love. Had I truly been ruthless with him, Andrew Gordon would be dead. I knew what I was doing."

"You were out of control."

"I was fully in control. He's alive because I allowed him to be." He rubbed a hand across the back of his neck in frustration. "I purposely held back. I was pulling my punches. I needed to convey a message, one he would never forget. Hurt my family and I will destroy you."

"What would you have done if he were a woman?"

He released her and took a step back to stare at her in surprise. "What? I've never raised a hand to any woman. Obviously, I would have responded differently. I've never been in a fight outside of the battlefield until today. I never even threw a punch during those stupid taproom brawls when Thad, Beast, and I were younger. How can you think I'd ever hurt a woman? Poppy, do you think I'd ever hurt you? Never you."

She seemed to look through him rather than at him. "Let's talk to Lavinia. She needs to be told everything before the Plimptons arrive."

She walked to her door and opened it to let him out. "You had better change out of your clothes first," she said quietly. "They're bloodied. So is your face. You ought to make yourself presentable before Lord and Lady Plimpton arrive." She glanced down at her gown. "I must do the same."

He ignored her when she tried to show him to the door. Instead, he took her hand and marched her down the hall toward

Lavinia's chamber. "And one more thing," he said when they reached Lavinia's door.

She met his steady gaze.

"I'd cut out my own heart sooner than hurt you."

But she looked at him as though he had already done irreparable harm. He had violated her trust and fallen off the pedestal she'd erected. She'd placed him on it ever since she was a little girl, and now he'd toppled off it.

He gave a curt, bitter laugh. "You want nothing to do with me anymore."

She shook her head in denial. "I don't know. I need time to think."

He did not bother to mask his disappointment. Poppy may have been shocked by the beating he'd given Andrew Gordon, but she was also jealous of Charlotte and afraid the girl had some magical hold on him. How was he to convince her there had never been any magic with Charlotte?

Sighing, he rapped at Lavinia's door.

Periwinkle gave a little bark as Lavinia's maid opened it to allow them in.

"Nathaniel? Poppy?" His aunt took one look at them, noted the spatters of blood and the grim looks on their faces, and quickly dismissed her maid. "What's happened?"

Nathaniel told her all.

It did not escape his notice that Lavinia reached out to grasp Poppy's hand while he delivered the dreadful news. Nor did it escape his notice that Poppy's gentle touch was soothing her as he dug deeper and tossed hard questions about Lady Plimpton and the young man who'd abandoned her with child.

"We were so innocent back then." She turned to smile at Poppy. "We were young and had no experience around men. The villain utterly dazzled us. All the girls in town were half in love with him. He was a captain in the army and his regiment had settled in Wellesford for the month before shipping off. I can't recall where they were sent. But we never saw or heard from him again."

"Did you ever learn what happened to him?" Poppy asked.

"Oh, my dear Poppy. I can see you hope for a satisfying resolution, but there was nothing romantic or tragic about that hound. He did not die heroically. He never proclaimed his undying love for my friend. He returned to England several years later and settled in the north with his wife. He was already married when he…when he came to Wellesford."

Poppy's hand went to her throat. "Oh, my goodness. What a deceitful toad. I'm so sorry for Lady Plimpton."

Lavinia sighed. "When she realized she was carrying his child, she came to me in tears. We didn't know what to do. Finally, we confided in my father. Your grandfather, Nathaniel. He was one of the wisest, kindest men who ever lived."

Poppy shot him a glance but quickly turned away when he returned her gaze. He knew what she was thinking. Until today, she'd thought of him the same way Lavinia had thought of his grandfather. Wise. Noble. Heroic. Now she thought of him as a barbarian. A man not worthy to be her test frog.

He turned back to Lavinia as she continued. "Your grandfather took charge at once."

"But he hid the news from her parents. You all did." Nathaniel gave a disapproving frown. "Don't you think they should have been told?"

"Perhaps, but Lady Plimpton's parents would not have treated her kindly. They called themselves devout, but they were cold and heartless. They would have beaten her and then disowned her. They would have tossed her onto the streets in disgrace and never allowed her into their home again. I suppose this is why she fell prey so easily to that young man's flattery. Her need for love."

Poppy's mouth was agape.

Of course, the Farthingales would never abandon their own. The notion that parents could be cruel to their children, kick them away and forget them, was inconceivable to her. This was yet another reason he was falling in love with Poppy. She would forgive her children's mistakes and love her grandchild whether or not legitimate.

To Poppy, a child was innocent and to be loved.

He cleared his throat. "How were you able to hide her condition?"

"My father arranged for her to join us on an extended trip, claiming I needed a companion and offering to pay all costs. Her family leaped at the offer. Their daughter traveling with an earl's family at no expense to themselves? They were gleeful."

Nathaniel was able to fill in the rest. "After the birth of her daughter, you returned to Wellesford and Grandfather made arrangements for Felicity to be baptized."

Lavinia nodded. "Lady Plimpton and I were there. Quietly in the background, of course. She needed to see her daughter given a name. My father took care of the rest, made certain Felicity was cared for properly. Shortly afterward, my friend met Lord Plimpton and fell utterly and truly in love with him. He's a good man."

"But he doesn't know her secret," Nathaniel said with a note of disapproval.

"No, he doesn't. They have their own children now. They've made a happy life for themselves. I'm not saying the situation is perfect or right. But Felicity is provided for and she was raised with care in the orphanage. Do not pass judgement on my friend, Nathaniel. We all make mistakes, some that are minor and some that will haunt us forever. It is her secret. We must respect it."

He gave a curt nod. "I will tell them about their nephew's forgery and nothing more. I have enough proof of this to have him locked away for the rest of his life. But I want him banished from England as soon as possible and forbidden to ever return."

He turned to Poppy in expectation.

"I think we're all agreed." Poppy glanced down at her stained gown and rose to leave. "We had better change out of our ruined clothes before the Plimptons arrive."

He went along with her and walked her back to her bedchamber, pausing at the door. There were so many things he wished to say to her, but she would listen to none of them while he stood before her with bloodied knuckles and the lingering urge to kill Andrew Gordon gleaming in his eyes.

"I'll pay for your gown, of course," he said. "We'll take care of it on our return to London. Have your modiste put the charge on my account."

She nodded.

He was about to turn away when she called to him, her voice little above a whisper. "Nathaniel, I'm glad you happened along when you did. I realize now Captain Gordon was planning something and I was about to become his next victim." She turned to him, no longer hiding the anguish in her eyes. "I think he'd been watching the three of us while we were having our tea."

Nathaniel's expression hardened, but he waited for Poppy to continue with the rest of it before he responded.

"He waited for Penelope and Olivia to leave. I was the isolated doe, and he was about to move in for the kill."

She blinked to stop the tears now gathering. "When you came along, he was busy telling me how ardently he admired me. It was a lie, of course. I suppose his intention was to lure me into an assignation. Once I was ruined, he'd have another stream of blackmail income from my parents." She emitted a mirthless laugh. "He must have thought I was from the wealthy side of the Farthingale clan. After all, why would any of you take me into your homes if I was poor as well as common?"

"Poppy…" Is this where her doubt sprang from? Her own belief that she was not worthy of his notice?

"I'm not angry with you, Nathaniel. I'm relieved. But I'm also angry with myself for being so defenseless. What if he meant to grab me right there? I had only a book as a weapon to fight him off. *Lady Cordelia's Tuscan Adventure*. That little book he could easily wrest from my hands. And then what?"

He wrapped her in his arms, not caring they were standing in the hallway and anyone could come along and see them. "Poppy, I'll never let anyone hurt you."

"I know. But you won't always be around to protect me, will

you? And I don't want to be helpless and in need of anyone's protection. I want to be able to fight off those scoundrels on my own."

"I've promised you this last day as your test frog. I'll finish my business with the Plimptons and then you and I will go out by the pond and I'll give you some battle training. But one evening isn't enough to make a warrior out of you. I don't want you getting overly confident and taking risks."

She shook her head and laughed. "Me? Too confident? I don't think that will be a problem."

He rubbed his thumb across her delicate cheek. "You're shy. That is your nature. Makes it all the more special when you offer your friendship, for it is a true friendship that comes with the promise of loyalty and trust. Penelope and Goose are fortunate to have you as a friend."

He wanted to kiss her, but his own heart had yet to calm, and the kiss would not be gentle or subdued.

Besides, he wasn't about to start something with the Plimptons about to arrive.

Nor would he start something while she was still trembling from the earlier incident.

He was not going to lose Poppy.

First, he needed to return to his chamber to make himself presentable.

Then, he needed to rid England of that vermin, Andrew Gordon.

Next, he would deal with Charlotte and her father.

After that…

"Nathaniel," Poppy said with an aching whisper, sliding her hand up his chest to rest it on his shoulder.

He bent his head to hers and did the very thing he'd promised himself not to do.

He kissed her.

And continued kissing her with all the love in his heart and promise in his soul.

It might not have been a perfect kiss, but it had conviction.

CHAPTER TWELVE

POPPY'S LIPS WERE still tingling and the butterflies in her stomach had yet to die down by the time she returned to Lavinia's quarters. Nathaniel hadn't said a word after he'd kissed her. He was now in his study speaking to Lord and Lady Plimpton. Thad and Beast still held their vile nephew somewhere within the house. She didn't know where they were keeping him, only that it was somewhere he could not escape. She doubted this charming manor had a dungeon. But if it did, no one deserved to inhabit it more than Captain Gordon.

Penelope and Goose had gone into town because arrangements still had to be made for the feeding and entertainment of this weekend's guests.

"Do come in, Poppy." Lavinia held out a hand to her. "Let's wait this out together."

Lavinia's quarters consisted of several rooms. Her bedchamber, her dressing room, and a sitting room that had a lavender silk settee for herself and a matching miniature settee for Periwinkle, her devoted dog. However, Periwinkle's favorite spot was on Lavinia's lap, and that's where he was comfortably perched when Poppy entered.

Lavinia motioned for Poppy to sit beside her. Periwinkle hopped onto her lap the moment she did so, rolling onto his back so that Poppy could scratch his belly. Lavinia shook her head and laughed. "He does love you best," she said with good-natured humor.

Poppy smothered a sigh.

She adored Periwinkle.

She loved Nathaniel.

But she was still overset by the beating he'd given Andrew Gordon. Yes, the cur deserved it. But what she'd seen in Nathaniel's eyes was so raw and savage, it had shocked her. And yet, it shouldn't have. *The Book of Love* spoke of these deeply embedded feelings. The most primal was a man's need to spread his seed. A step above that was the need to protect his family. *Protect them so they would not be eaten by wolves.*

Also, she was overset that Charlotte would arrive tomorrow. What if the beautiful duke's daughter was able to rekindle Nathaniel's passion? After all, he must have felt something for her if he'd...

She dismissed the unsettling thought and returned her attention to Lavinia.

Lavinia withdrew her lace handkerchief and dabbed it at the corners of her eyes. "What a mess this is. At least the wretched villain will be out of our lives forever."

Poppy grunted. "He almost destroyed his aunt and doesn't even know it. Hopefully, she will never realize we know her secret. He thought he was destroying you, that Felicity was your daughter."

"And I will claim her as my own if word somehow gets out. I have nothing to lose while my friend risks losing everything. I will never allow it to happen."

"The one who loses in all of this is Felicity Billings. It seems cruel not to tell her," Poppy said. "She's so alone in the world."

"She won't be any more. We'll make her feel welcome." Lavinia frowned thoughtfully. "Who knows if there ever will be a good moment to speak to her about this delicate subject? It isn't up to us to tell her the truth. I know it seems harsh to you, Poppy."

She nodded. "It does."

"The choice is Lady Plimpton's. I won't have a hand in destroying my friend's reputation or her happy marriage."

"No, of course not. I understand there is no easy answer. Lady Plimpton will be hurt if the truth comes out. Felicity will always wonder who she belongs to if it doesn't."

"Yes, but she's a cheerful young woman with much of her life ahead of her. Who's to say she won't find a fine man to marry and raise a family of their own? I'm relieved she isn't a part of this scoundrel's schemes."

By early evening, Andrew Gordon's regimental commander had been contacted and arrangements made to resign his commission before getting him out of England. Beast and Thad had gone along to ensure he was put on a ship to distant shores. Their mission would take more than an evening, perhaps more than an entire day, but Beast had assured Olivia they would be back in time for the weekend party.

"I'll miss you every moment," he'd told Goose, earning groans from Thad, and mutters from Nathaniel about the fall of man, for Beast was obviously leg-shackled to Goose and delighted about it.

Poppy sighed and thought it splendid that such a sweeping love could exist. She wanted this with Nathaniel, but wasn't certain it could happen. She'd felt passion in his kisses. Was this passion for her alone? Or did he feel the same when kissing other women?

The household calmed down once Thad and Beast rode off with Captain Gordon.

Nathaniel finished his business with the Plimptons and the local magistrate.

That evening, Lavinia chose to take her supper in her quarters, leaving only the five of them at the dining table. Poppy and her friends, and Pip and Nathaniel. Pip, who was seated across the table from Poppy, began to stare at her intently.

She took a sip of her leek soup, then set down her spoon. "What is it, Pip?"

He appeared distressed as he allowed his own spoon to clatter onto his soup bowl. "Was your love letter a fake? Is it true, you don't have a beau?"

Poppy sighed. "No beau."

Pip nodded. "Don't be sad. I'll marry you, Poppy."

Nathaniel choked on his wine. "Pip, I don't think–"

Poppy cast the boy a gentle smile. "That is very kind of you, Pip. But I'm not sad. Andrew Gordon was a cheat and a forger. I'm glad we found out about his deceitful nature as soon as we did. As for your proposal, I am honored. But you know I cannot accept."

He nodded. "I'll ask you again when I'm older."

Her heart was touched by his innocent earnestness. "I doubt you'll find me very appealing by then, but thank you."

Penelope, who was seated beside the boy, patted his hand. "Poppy will likely be married by the time you're all grown up. I think she'll want you to find a girl closer to your own age."

He groaned and made a wincing face. "But they're all silly."

"You'll like them better when you're older." Nathaniel cleared his throat. "Goose, are you certain you don't want to stay over this evening? Your old bedchamber is available. I'm sure Beast will feel more comfortable knowing you're with your friends."

She shook her head and smiled. "I'll be fine at Gosling Hall. My staff will look after me."

"We can walk you over after supper," Penelope said. "It's a lovely evening. Pip, do you want to join us?"

The boy's eyes lit up. "Yes. May I, Nathaniel?"

He nodded. "Of course."

They were all subdued as they walked Goose across the meadow to Gosling Hall. The light had just begun to fade and it cast a golden glow across the meadow. A moist heat lingered in the air. A family of deer grazed at the edge of the meadow.

Poppy walked with her two friends. Nathaniel and Pip strolled at a leisurely pace ahead of them. The two of them appeared to be engaged in an enthralling conversation.

Nathaniel's head was bowed toward the boy as he listened to him chatter. Poppy's heart tugged when she saw Pip's eyes widen in adoration as Nathaniel responded. There was such honesty in the boy's feelings. He admired Nathaniel. In turn, Nathaniel was patient and attentive to his barrage of questions. He obviously loved Pip. The affection he showed the boy was such a stark contrast to the savagery he'd shown Andrew Gordon.

She had yet to reconcile the two sides of Nathaniel.

Or was she making too much of it? When pushed to protect his family, would her father have behaved any differently? Even for herself, what would she have done if someone threatened her family? As much of an observer as she was, she'd fight to save them. She would never allow anyone to hurt her loved ones.

Indeed, wasn't she angry with herself for never learning anything of the art of defense? Nathaniel was going to teach her some tricks as soon as they returned to Sherbourne Manor and sent Pip off to bed. Since it was Penelope's turn to read the boy a story, Nathaniel was free to tutor her then.

"Poppy, we're running out of time," Penelope said in a whisper, holding her back while her brother and Pip walked ahead. "There's only one night left before we're descended upon by Nathaniel's London friends. Can you win Nathaniel's heart by then?"

She shook her head. "Perhaps, but that isn't the right question."

Penelope quirked her head, peering at her in confusion. "It isn't? Then what is?"

"I may win his heart tonight. But will Charlotte steal it back tomorrow?"

Penelope groaned. "No. Never. I refuse to consider the possibility."

But Poppy had to, for her own heart was at stake and Nathaniel had the power to crush it.

"A MAN HAS certain sensitive spots on his body," Nathaniel said, turning Poppy to face him as they stood beside the pond in the last glimmers of daylight. There was a light breeze blowing off the water toward them, one strong enough to keep the pesky gnats from swarming around them and biting their skin.

They'd go for Poppy first, for her skin was sweeter.

Soft and sweet.

But he shook out of the thought. He'd brought Poppy out here in the amber glow of twilight because the grass was thick and soft and he didn't want her hurt if she tripped and fell. Not that he would ever purposely harm her, but defense required feints and lunging and quickness of feet. It was not uncommon for an untrained warrior to get his feet tangled and take a fall.

He would be gentle with Poppy, of course.

But not so gentle that she'd learn nothing.

He cleared his throat. "Everyone has certain sensitive spots. The eyes. The throat."

Poppy nodded. "Nathaniel, you are blushing."

"I am not. It's just that..." He raked a hand through his hair, knowing he could not skirt the issue. "A man is also sensitive in the area between his legs."

She grinned. "You already look pained."

And she hadn't even struck him there yet. Not that he wanted her to, but he wanted her to know it was a potential spot. The best spot to strike if a young lady wished to take down a male attacker. "Hitting a man *there* with sufficient force will drop him to his knees in agony."

"Interesting." She stared at the spot, which caused him to respond with agony of quite a different sort.

Lord, what was he thinking?

The girl was making him brainless again.

He put his arms on her shoulders and turned her away from

him so that she was now facing the water and not his tightening loins. "Now, if a man approaches you from behind. You must–"

"Is that it? Am I to learn no more about the vulnerable spot between your legs?"

Lord Almighty.

"There's nothing more to say. You hit a man there with all your might and run." He held her firm and kept her turned away from him. "Now, if a man comes at you from behind." He started to put his arms around her, inhaled her lavender scent, and absorbed her soft body now lightly pressed against his, and stopped.

Hell, this wasn't working out.

What had he been thinking when he offered to tutor her in the art of defense? "I'm going to give you a pistol. Hide it on your person."

As he relaxed his grip, she turned to face him. "Where?" she asked, rolling her eyes and motioning downward toward her gown.

It hugged her body, outlining her magnificent curves. And she still wore the necklace that plunged beneath the fabric in the valley of her breasts.

He was a nitwit. His gaze shot straight there even though he knew it shouldn't. He'd read *The Book of Love*. He understood the science behind his responses. Yet, he was still responding. And aching. "Doesn't matter where you hide it. If someone comes after you, take out the pistol and shoot him."

She cast him one of those rare and magnificent Poppy Farthingale dimpled smiles. She knew she had him on her hook. She knew he was helplessly dangling and unable to break away. She'd caught him.

However, her smile was not one of triumph. It was one of sheer love.

He groaned in agony.

He needed to marry this girl for the sake of his own sanity.

He needed her beside him for all the days of his life. "Poppy, damn it. Will you–"

The rattle of carriages rolling through the manor gate and up the drive distracted them from this magical moment, although starting a marriage proposal with "Poppy, damn it" might not have been his cleverest move. "Hellfire, they've arrived early."

Poppy looked crestfallen.

He took her hand and gave it a light squeeze to assure her all would turn out well. But what if it didn't? Not that he had any doubts about his feelings for Poppy, but these friends were not going to accept her so easily.

They weren't friends such as Beast and Thad were. They would not stand beside him and support him to their dying breath. No, these were his Upper Class acquaintances who would look upon Poppy as his dalliance, unable to conceive that he would prefer a merchant's daughter over the daughter of a wealthy and powerful duke. "We'd better head back to greet them."

She hesitated. "You go on ahead. I'd like to stay out here a little while longer. I'll be back before dark. You needn't worry about me."

Of course, he'd worry.

But to appear with Poppy by his side would force a confrontation with Charlotte before the carriage wheels had rolled to a stop. "Very well."

He greeted the duke and Charlotte who were the first to step down from their carriage. "Welles," Charlotte said, casting him a jaded, let's-have-sex-tonight pout, "our journey was beastly and we are all famished."

"I'll have Cook prepare something for you." He turned to the duke, arching an eyebrow in question. Why had they arrived a day early?

The old man cleared his throat. "I hope you don't mind. I thought my daughter could do with a good dose of country air. London is a little stale at the moment."

"Lady Hawksworth is a jealous, old biddy and spread malicious lies about me. If she weren't so old and withered, and a lady, but in name only, for we all know that she is common and no amount of fine clothes or titles will change that. The point is, if she were a man, my father would have called her out."

He didn't bother to ask what Charlotte had done. No doubt the poor woman had caught Charlotte in a compromising position with her husband, Lord Hawksworth. The man was old, not particularly handsome, but his marriage to Lady Hawksworth had been considered a successful one. Perhaps not a love match in the fiery, passionate sense, but one in an abiding friendship sense.

He could see by the amused gleam in Charlotte's eyes, she had considered it a lark to destroy their loving bond.

Lord, what had he done?

Charlotte wouldn't hesitate to set about destroying Poppy next.

He turned to greet his other guests. Although most were mere acquaintances, there were some decent souls among them. He liked Thomas Halford, the Earl of Wycke. He'd brought his sister, Anne Halford, and his mother, Countess Wycke, with him. They would be pleasant company, for all three of them were jovial and good-natured. They would get along well with Penelope and Poppy.

Also present were Lord March and Lord Jameson, bachelor friends of his. They often made the round of parties together, and while Nathaniel would sometimes join them afterward in the gaming hells and other entertainments, he'd long ago grown bored with these outings and rarely joined them now. But March and Jameson still enjoyed their freedoms and indulged in them a little too heavily for Nathaniel's liking.

They weren't bad or immoral men. However, he would not like them getting too friendly with Poppy or his sister. They had some reforming to do. He'd have to watch those two.

He'd invited a few other prominent, *ton* families, social acquaintances of Lavinia's who also were well acquainted with Charlotte and her father because they all traveled in the best circles.

Within the hour, his guests were all settled in their chambers and assigned maids and valets to assist them in changing out of their travel clothes. Those who were hungry would soon come down for the light repast his cook had hastily cobbled together. Soames had overseen the setting of the dinner table in all its finery and made certain his footmen were in their livery, ready to serve the lords and ladies as they sat down to dine.

Nathaniel had a few minutes to spare before the horde migrated downstairs. He went in search of Poppy, needing to make certain she'd returned to the house. But it was more than that. He wanted her under his protection, not only from his bachelor friends, but also from those who would cast her condescending glances.

He had just stepped into the entry hall when he spotted her coming out of his library with a book in hand.

She smiled when she saw him, which eased his heart tremendously. "What have you there?"

"A book on travels to Tuscany."

He groaned, for the damn book she was reading about the fictional Lady Cordelia's adventures in Tuscany was putting ideas into her head. It was worse than *The Book of Love*, which had scientific merit. But the Tuscan adventure was nothing more than an illicit, sexual romp.

His thoughts must have been obvious, for she put her hand on his arm and cast him another gentle smile. "Lady Cordelia married her count. They fell in love and lived happily ever after in his Tuscan castle. He did do naughty things to her and with her before they married." She tipped her head up and regarded him with a steady gaze. "But he loved her, and she knew it. She was no mere dalliance to him. It just took her a little longer to trust her own feelings and admit she loved him."

"And you, Poppy. What are you feeling?"

He felt her fingers tense on his arm, but he never found out her response, for his guests began to make their way downstairs before he received an answer from her.

Poppy quickly released his arm and skittered up the servants' stairs.

Damn it.

She wasn't the hired help.

He wanted her to stand beside him.

He wanted to proudly introduce her to one and all as his betrothed.

He supposed he ought to propose to her first, actually get the words out instead of merely think them.

Charlotte came toward him and took his arm. "Will you escort me into the dining hall?" She purposely leaned into him so that her breast rubbed against his arm.

"Charlotte, stop it."

She drew back in surprise. "Stop what?"

He worried that he'd been too abrupt with her, but she appeared impatient and annoyed rather than hurt. He was interfering with her game and she didn't like it. That's all he was to her, a game to relieve her boredom.

But he also wanted her to know the blackmailer was no longer a threat. Looking at her now, he wondered whether she had ever been blackmailed.

He shook his head and sighed. "What do you know of a man named Andrew Gordon?"

She paled and drew her hand off him. "Why do you ask?"

"He's been run out of England. He will never threaten you again."

"Threaten me?" She blinked and shook her head. "What makes you think he and I have anything to do with each other?"

He shrugged. "I don't know. But I felt it was important you were made aware. You seemed to be unhappy. You struck me as desperate to–"

"Desperate? How dare you!" She gave a theatrical toss of her hair and her eyes blazed as though outraged.

"Cut out the mock indignation, Charlotte. You'll draw attention to yourself. I'm not the one with something to hide. But I think you are. Do you want my help or not?"

She ignored the question and walked into the dining room ahead of him.

If she was overset by what he'd told her, she didn't show it. Indeed, she put on an ovation-worthy act, tossing a dazzling smile at any man who would look her way, and they all did.

She reveled in their besotted responses.

Having read *The Book of Love*, he understood the gleam in every man's eye. Charlotte was the fertile female they all desired. They were welcome to her. Looking at her now, Nathaniel wondered how he'd ever found her appealing. He'd succumbed to her charms only the one time, the day he'd been to the docks and seen those coffins lined up. He'd arrived at Lord Angstrom's ball drunk and continued drinking in order to numb his pain.

But when sober, he'd never trusted Charlotte. He may have been attracted by her beauty, but never enchanted. Her affected pout had never drawn him in.

However, despite having absorbed the science in that book, having read and reread it from front to back and memorized several of its passages, he still found women confusing.

Why wasn't Charlotte relieved to no longer be under threat from Andrew Gordon?

She was acting oddly.

He shook his head and sighed, knowing he'd done what he thought was right. He'd tried to protect her from that villain.

Even Poppy confounded him, and she was the most open and honest girl he'd ever met. Not that she was purposely trying to confuse him. She was doing nothing but being helpful. In truth, she had done nothing to lure him. She hadn't used a single spell or trick or recipe, or whatever one wanted to call the advice in that book.

She had *given* him the book to read.

Yet, he still responded to her like a low-brained simpleton, even more so now.

He took his seat at the head of the dining table. Penelope took the seat opposite his and was as charming and delightful a hostess as he could ever have hoped. She engaged their guests and asked after their travels. Even listened to their petulant complaints with compassion.

Lord Wycke passed him a whispered comment. "Your sister is charming, Welles. I understand this is her first year out. She'll be married off quickly." He laughed and shook his head. "I might do it myself. She's utterly delightful."

Nathaniel merely nodded.

Perhaps Penelope was only obstinate and defiant with him.

And Thad, of course.

Lord, she tortured Thad.

Penelope delightful? He loved his sister, but he wasn't blind to her faults. *Stubborn. Rabid, at times. Often up to mischief.* He'd be relieved when she fell in love and found someone else to torment.

Lavinia came down a few minutes later escorted by Poppy. Whatever pleasure he felt at the mere sight of Poppy was shattered when Charlotte's father passed a comment. "You allow your aunt's companion at your dinner table, Welles? Quite extraordinary." He made no effort to be discreet or civil.

"Miss Farthingale is not Lavinia's companion." Nathaniel fisted his hands to stem his anger. "She's a valued guest in my home."

"A dear friend to all of us," Penelope responded similarly. "Our families have been close friends for years. Do come sit next to me, Miss Farthingale."

Lord Jameson leered at her. "There's an empty seat beside me as well."

She thanked him and sat beside Penelope. While seating order would be adhered to more formally tomorrow and through the weekend, this repast was set out for anyone who wished to come down to dine and therefor the arrangements were casual.

Lord Jameson came around to sit on the other side of her. "Are you anything like those sisters of yours? I hear you're all named after flowers. The eldest girls did quite well for themselves."

"I believe you are referring to my cousins. And yes, we are named after flowers."

"Soft and beautiful," he murmured.

"Intelligent and compassionate, I hope. We are neither delicate nor mere ornaments to adorn a man's arm. I fully expect my cousin, Lily, to become the first female Fellow in the Royal Society."

"I daresay she will not," the Duke of Winthrow intoned. "Impertinent, ill-mannered girl. I shall never cast my vote for her."

"Why not, Your Grace? Oh, I know she's young still and only beginning her scientific research in earnest. But in time, you'll recognize her brilliance and be as proud of her as we all are."

Lord Jameson drained his glass of wine and held it out for a footman to pour more. "And what is your flower, Miss Farthingale?"

"Poppy."

Nathaniel emitted a soft growl, not liking the way Jameson was looking at her. As though he wished to pluck her petals.

Over his dead body.

Or rather, Jameson would be the one found dead if he ever laid a hand on Poppy.

Penelope guided the conversation to safer ground, reviewing tomorrow's planned entertainments. "Tea and archery for the ladies. Riding and hunting for the men."

"But what's to be our sport for this evening?" Lord March asked, turning to Poppy. "I'll deem it an honor to partner with you, whatever game it is."

"Welles, I claim you," Charlotte said.

By her tone, Nathaniel knew she meant it in more ways than a genteel party game. He'd talk to Charlotte later. "We'll play whist." He ordered Soames to set up card tables in the salon.

He partnered with Charlotte for no other reason than to keep her from menacing Poppy. To his surprise, Poppy appeared to be handling Jameson and March quite well without any assistance from him.

The men were behaving themselves, but for how long?

"Welles, do pay attention," Charlotte said with marked impatience. "It's your turn."

The card games ended well past midnight, and his guests finally retired to their chambers.

Nathaniel was tired and eager for sleep by the time he closed up the house and returned to his quarters. As he entered, he realized he was not alone. Charlotte was naked in his bed. "Let the real sport begin," she purred, beckoning him to her.

As she motioned to him, the sheet slipped down to expose her breasts.

His low brain didn't respond.

He wasn't surprised.

Having made his choice, he had moved beyond the primitive brain function. Poppy was the girl he wanted.

"With your father next door? I don't think so." He reached for the nightgown she'd tossed on the floor. "Get dressed. Go back to your own room. Don't come in here again."

She tipped her head as though confused. "Will you join me in my room?"

"No. Not tonight. Not tomorrow. Not ever. Play with someone else, Charlotte."

"It's *her*. You want her." Her gold curls fell over her bare shoulders as she tossed her head back in indignation. "I see. She's your bed mate now and I've interrupted your party."

"Nothing of the sort." He handed her the nightgown and repeated his request to put it on.

She grabbed it out of his hands and donned it. "You'll regret this."

Oh, he already regretted inviting her and her father. It was his punishment for being too arrogant and pigheaded to see the treasure in front of him. Poppy had always been there. All he had to do was look.

He would pay for it now. Charlotte would see to it.

He walked to the door and eased it open. "Hallway's clear. Leave now."

She cast him a malicious grin and strolled out.

He watched her saunter down the hall, but instead of entering her guest chamber, she knocked on the door next to it. "Miss Farthingale, I need your help."

Poppy must have been awake and not yet in bed, for she quickly opened her door. "What is it, Lady Charlotte? I..." She caught sight of Charlotte in her scanty nightgown and then noticed him standing with his arms crossed over his chest by his door.

Charlotte cast him a gloating smile before turning to Poppy. "He's delicious, isn't he? I hope you don't mind sharing him with me this weekend. But rest assured, he is mine. He will marry me and then you will no longer be welcome here."

Charlotte hurried into her room as Nathaniel stalked down the hall to put an end to the foolishness.

Poppy stared at him, her mouth agape.

"You can't possibly believe I invited her into my bedchamber."

Poppy shut the door in his face.

Chapter Thirteen

Poppy ignored the soft knocks at her door while she took a deep breath and then another to steady herself. "Go away, Nathaniel."

She didn't believe he had invited Charlotte into his bed.

But Charlotte had gone there anyway.

Nathaniel had tossed her out, but how many other girls like Charlotte would come along? Would Nathaniel be as adamant in booting them out of his bedchamber? In her heart, she knew the answer. Yes, he would boot them out. Once he was married, he would never be unfaithful to his wife.

But could she be that wife?

She'd watched Penelope and seen how effortlessly she'd entertained their guests, how unruffled she appeared to be by their early arrival. Goose would have managed with equal ease. They were to the manor born.

But she hadn't been.

She was a merchant's daughter, and his Society friends were wondering what she was doing here.

She sank onto her bed, feeling defeated. And angry with herself for giving up so easily. And angrier with herself for not understanding that she was an outsider and not likely to be accepted in the finer circles without a battle.

Well, if her cousins had managed it, so could she.

She lit a candle to cast some light as she began to pack her things, intending only to move across the meadow to Gosling Hall for the weekend. She wasn't running away so much as freeing Nathaniel from the burden of having to defend her presence here to his friends.

Moonlight filtered into her bedchamber so that the clash of amber candlelight and silver moonlight gave the room a magical glow. She'd spent her summers in this room ever since she was a little girl. She loved it here and it saddened her to leave even for a few days.

She had no intention of imposing on Goose and Beast beyond the weekend. Of course, they would invite her to stay for as long as she wished. It wouldn't be long, just until Nathaniel's friends returned to London.

She tried to convince herself it was for the best.

She didn't fit in.

Lord Wycke and his family weren't so bad, but they were the only ones she could abide. Lord Jameson and Lord March had gawked and leered at her all evening. Charlotte and her father had looked down their noses at her, and when they were not sneering at her, they were pointedly ignoring her.

His other friends did nothing but complain. First about their travels, then about the hastily prepared food they had been served. Never mind they'd appeared unannounced, and poor Cook had been on her feet since early morning working diligently to prepare for tomorrow's festivities and the grand party on Saturday evening.

The hastily prepared food was delicious. Nathaniel's friends still found fault with it. When they weren't complaining, they were speaking of their horses and phaetons or going on about the difficulty in finding decent servants.

Not once did they speak of weighty topics.

There was no mention of the soldiers returning from war who needed to be fed and housed. Nor did they concern themselves with the widows and children of soldiers who'd died in battle.

She understood this was a weekend party and did not expect them to engage in important conversations, but to show not a whit of compassion for anyone other than themselves was too much for her to bear.

Not once did they acknowledge her, for they'd taken their cues from the Winthrows and were not going to accept her as one of them. In truth, she hoped never to become like them.

Before retiring, she made it a point to go to the kitchen and personally thank Nathaniel's staff.

She couldn't help it.

She was not so far removed from the Sherbourne servants.

Merchant's daughter. Charlotte and her father had gone to great lengths to remind her of her station.

She was about to douse her candle and retire to bed when she noticed someone had slid a note under her door. She crossed the room and picked up the square of white paper off the floor. *Meet me in the library. N.*

Sighing, she tossed the note on her bed, donned her robe and slippers, and then picked up her candle to light the way as she walked downstairs in search of Nathaniel.

She did owe him an explanation for why she was moving to Gosling Hall in the morning. Also, she wished to assure him that she was not angry with him and she trusted him.

Instead of Nathaniel, she was surprised to find Lord Jameson standing in the library. He'd removed his jacket, vest, and cravat. His elegant shirt, made of the finest lawn, Savile Row, no doubt, was untucked and open to reveal his hairy chest. If he thought that a dark spray of hair against ghostly pale skin was appealing to her, then he was sadly mistaken. "Come to me, my little minx."

He reached out to take her in his arms, but she skittered behind one of Nathaniel's sturdy leather chairs. "Are you mad? What are you doing here?"

He lunged for her, but she darted behind Nathaniel's desk. "Don't play coy. You asked me to meet you here."

Poppy gasped. "No, I didn't. I assure you most heartily, I did not."

He stopped chasing her and frowned. "You wrote me a note."

She shook her head, realizing they'd both been set up. "No, it's a trick. We've been played for fools. Get out quickly, my lord. Someone is about to walk in on us and expose us as lovers. So, unless you wish to be married to a woman with little dowry, then I suggest you gather your clothes and climb out the window as fast as you can."

"You have no money?"

"Sadly, no. I'm the poor relation everyone pities."

He cast her a wry grin. "Miss Farthingale, you are too beautiful to pity and you would not get me to run if my circumstances were other than what they are. Unfortunately, I am in need of an heiress."

"Then disappear quickly, Lord Jameson. I hear footsteps down the stairs."

He gathered his clothes in his arms and made it out the window a few moments before Nathaniel burst in. He glanced around and saw she was standing alone. "Thank goodness," he murmured, running a hand raggedly through his hair. He shut the door behind him and then started toward her.

She noticed he had also shed his jacket, vest, and cravat, but he cut a much finer figure than Lord Jameson. His shirt was neatly tucked in and the fine lawn fabric hugged his muscled arms and enhanced the broadness of his chest. "Are you all right?" he asked.

She nodded. "I thought you'd sent me a note asking me to meet you here."

He frowned. "I didn't."

"Then what brought you down here?"

"I knocked at your door." He arched an eyebrow. "The one you slammed in my face."

She winced. "I'm sorry."

"Don't be." He cupped her face, his manner achingly gentle. "I should have expected her mischief. But I didn't want you thinking the worst. I returned to your room in the hope you would allow me to explain. Then I got worried when you didn't respond to my knock. I walked in and saw the note on your bed." He looked around once again. "I thought Charlotte had set you up to be ruined."

"She had. You'll be pleased to know your friend she intended to set up with me is not as depraved as Charlotte believes."

He frowned. "Which friend?"

"I'm not going to tell you yet. He didn't harm me. He didn't set a hand on me. I had no need to use the tricks of defense you taught me, but I would have if the need arose." She cast him a look of pride. "Fingers to the eyes. Fist to the throat. Knee to his… delicate parts."

"Poppy, don't protect him from me."

"I'm not. He didn't do anything. I won't have you pounding an innocent man to dust as you did that villain, Captain Gordon."

"Other than that wastrel Gordon, I am not in the habit of using my fists to resolve disputes. Was he dressed?"

Heat immediately rose in her cheeks. *Drat*, she was blushing. Why couldn't she be aloof and mysterious? But no, she was expressive. She gave everything away. "He had on his shirt and pants, just like you."

"Buttoned?"

Her eyes suddenly rounded in alarm. "Nathaniel! If I've been set up to be ruined, then you're the one they'll find with me." She shoved at his solid chest. "You must go."

He laughed and folded his arms across his chest. "No."

She may as well have been pushing against a brick wall. "Stubborn man, why won't you budge? Don't you understand? You'll be forced to marry me."

He nodded. "I understand perfectly. But no one will force me."

"Of course, they will. The Farthingales? Are you serious? There'll be a hundred rifles pointed at your throat. And that's just my family. Beast and Thad will hold you down at the altar if they must. Penelope will shoot you between the eyes if you don't."

He turned and latched the door, then propped a chair against it for good measure. "No one will disturb us now."

"Nathaniel, are you not listening to me?"

He strode to the window and drew the curtains shut. "Hearing your every word, my love."

"Your–" She shook her head, confused. "What did you just call me?"

He grinned. "You heard me. Or were you not *listening* to me?"

"I've been listening, looking, and finally thinking. This isn't the sort of life I want, Nathaniel. I don't mean you or Penelope or Goose. I love all of you. Lavinia, Thad, Beast, and Pip, too. These summers have been idyllic, but they're not real. Being called Lavinia's companion and questioned about my place at the table, that's real."

"You have it backward."

"Do I?" She meant to say something more, but forgot what it was. Nathaniel now had her in his arms and was trailing hot kisses down her neck. "Nathaniel," she said in a breathy whisper and *eeped*.

"No one will dare look down their noses at you once you're my countess."

"Your countess?" *Oh, goodness!* He trailed more kisses along her shoulder, nudging her robe aside so that her skin was laid bare.

"Marry me, Poppy."

"Marry you?" She stared at him, stunned.

He stopped kissing her and returned her steady gaze. As the silence persisted between them, he smiled and caressed her cheek. "You're doing that thing again."

"What thing?"

"Thinking too hard. Trying to be logical when all you ought to be doing is feeling. Do you want to marry me or not? Do you love me or not? You're the one who read *The Book of Love* first.

What are you feeling, Poppy?"

"Um, quite splendid." She licked her lips. "And warm. Very warm. Hot, actually." She was only wearing her nightgown and robe, which happened to be off her shoulder at the moment while he nuzzled her. She expected her robe would soon come off. If he didn't take it off her, she'd fling it off herself, for the heat of his hands as he stroked them up and down her arms was exquisitely delightful.

His touch burned into her soul.

He began to remove the pins in her hair. She closed her eyes as he slowly slid his hands through the wild tumble of her unbound hair. "What else do you feel, Poppy?"

He cupped her breast.

Why was it so hot in here? Every pulse in her body began to throb. "Oh, goodness."

Before she knew it, he'd unfastened the ties of her robe.

"You're removing my clothes."

"I said I would once I was ready to marry you. But are you ready to marry me?"

She closed her eyes. There was nothing between her breast and his hand but a thin layer of cotton. A seductress would have worn silk. But no, she had on sturdy cotton.

His mouth closed over the tip of her breast, his tongue licking through the fabric.

She pressed his head against her chest, certain she would expire if he stopped doing this magical thing to her with his lips and tongue. "Nathaniel. Oh, heavens. Your touch."

He eased off her breast and kissed her softly on the lips. "It's you I want to hold in the moonlight. Marry me."

"Marry you?"

"It's your body I want beside mine in bed. It's your smile I want to see across from me at the breakfast table."

"Did you say marry you?"

"Twice now, I believe." He kissed her again, his lips gentle against hers. "It's you I trust with my secrets and my cares. It's you I trust with my heart. So, I'm giving it to you, wholly and completely, and I shall never take it back. It's yours forever."

The breath left her in a rush. "Nathaniel."

He smiled wryly. "Is that a yes?"

She laughed. "I've loved you from the first moment I ever set eyes on you. I've never stopped loving you. I gave my heart to you long ago. I was afraid to admit it to myself or to you until now."

"I'm sorry, Poppy. I didn't make it easy for you. I was an arrogant–"

"No, you weren't about to notice a little girl."

"You grew up nicely." He grinned and kissed her again on the mouth. "Is it a yes, Poppy?"

She nodded. "It's always been yes."

His gaze turned fiery. "I'm so sorry I took so long to *see* you."

"It happened when it was meant to happen. And what do you see when you look at me now?"

He grinned. "Fertile female with healthy breasts." Then his grin faded. "So much more than that. My confidant. My partner in life. My happiness. My starlight."

Her heart began to pound through her ears as he slowly slipped the nightgown off her body so there was nothing between her skin and his touch. His mouth closed over her breast and his tongue began a teasing swirl across its taut bud.

The pounding in her ears grew louder.

Nathaniel groaned and pulled away. He drew the nightgown back in place. He gathered her robe and wrapped it properly around her. "Lord, you're beautiful."

Her brain was in a muddle. "Why did you put my clothes back on me?"

"That pounding you hear isn't your heart, Poppy." He cast her a tender smile. "It's the door."

She felt foolish.

He kissed her again. "I love you. Are you ready for the fireworks display?"

He secured the ties of her robe and then strode to the door to open it. Charlotte and her father were there, Charlotte's face already twisted in a gloating smirk that turned to surprise and then outrage when she realized he and not some other hapless lord had thrown open the door. "What trick is this?"

Lord Wycke, his mother, Penelope, and Lavinia stood behind the Winthrows. Poppy thought she heard them cheering. Lurking further back on the stairs were Lord Jameson and Lord March who were laughing, although Poppy suspected their glee was for Charlotte's set down and not for her own ruination.

Then marching in the front door to add to the din were Beast, Goose, and Thad. "What's going on?" Beast asked.

Periwinkle barked for joy and wriggled out of Lavinia's arms. He ran first to Goose to greet her and then ran to Poppy.

She bent to lift him into her arms. "There's a good boy." She scratched him behind the ears.

Yes, even the beasts adored Poppy's touch.

Nathaniel stepped back to allow them all in. "A celebration is in order. Miss Farthingale has just consented to be my wife."

His sister shrieked and threw herself into his arms. "Thank you, Nathaniel."

He laughed. "Loopy, I did it for me, not for you."

"I don't care." She wiped the tears streaming down her cheeks. "I love you, Nathaniel. I'm so happy for you and Poppy. I couldn't ask for a nicer sister."

Periwinkle was caught between them as Penelope and Goose threw their arms around Poppy. "The book worked," Goose whispered. "It really is magic."

Poppy nodded. "Penelope, you're next."

Beast looked on, bemused.

Thad looked stricken. "Och, Nathaniel. What have ye done?"

He grinned. "Fallen madly in love, it seems."

After the rounds of congratulations, most of the guests returned to their quarters, but Nathaniel requested Winthrow and his daughter to remain behind. Poppy was surprised that he meant to address the matter of Charlotte's note now instead of waiting until morning. She supposed there was no point in delay.

"What is the meaning of this, Welles?" the duke intoned.

Poppy stood by Nathaniel's side, feeling it was important to remain. She was not one for confrontation, but a proper countess would not back away from this problem. If Nathaniel appeared surprised, he did not show it as he responded. "There are a few loose ends to tie up before we all retire to our beds." He held out the note Charlotte had slid under her door. "Your Grace, do you notice something odd about it?"

"No, should I have?"

"It is Charlotte's handwriting."

"What if it is?" But he held his hands out in a placating gesture. "Now, Welles. There's no harm done. You obviously care for Miss Farthingale, so it all turned out well. Perhaps your offer of marriage to her came a bit sooner than you intended, but it is obvious your proposal was in the offing."

"The problem is serious," Nathaniel countered. "Do you know a man by the name of Andrew Gordon?"

Charlotte paled. "We've never heard of him." She took her father's arm. "Come along, Father. This is all nonsense."

"Stay put, Charlotte," Nathaniel said, his tone sharp and commanding.

Her father took her arm when she attempted to leave. "He said, stay. What's this about?"

"I believe your daughter and Andrew Gordon are involved in blackmail schemes. Friends of ours have been receiving threatening letters. Pay up or we'll expose your dirty secrets. I caught the man forging my name, pretending to act on my behalf while digging up dirt for them to use to destroy lives."

Charlotte's gaze turned venomous. "He's lying, Father!"

"How do you explain this, Charlotte? The handwriting on the

note you slipped under Miss Farthingale's door is the same as on the blackmail note one of my friends received."

"Your friend? Hah! It was your aunt, Lavinia. And I know her secret. Harm me and I shall reveal it to the world. She'll be ruined. Destroyed. Have no doubt that I shall do it."

Her father gazed at her in horror. "Charlotte!"

She turned her seething rage on her father. "What did you expect me to do once you cut off my allowance? Remain by your side? The dutiful daughter? Marry a dullard and live under his thumb? Pretend to enjoy my wifely duties? I want none of that."

Her father was too shocked to respond, so Nathaniel filled in the rest of it. "When Andrew Gordon approached you, attempting to blackmail you, instead you offered to work with him. You traveled in the highest circles. You'd give him access to the wealthiest men in England."

She laughed. "Women, too."

Nathaniel looked disgusted. "Of course, forgive me for assuming you had a whit of remorse. Widows and orphans were not off limits." He turned to her father. "Andrew Gordon has been shipped out of England, someplace far where he can never touch anyone here again. I'll leave your daughter's fate to you. But if she attempts to—"

"She won't. I give you my word of honor."

Poppy had never seen a man look more defeated. Nor a young woman more scared, for Charlotte obviously feared her father. "What will you do to her, Your Grace?" The words were out of her mouth before she could stop herself.

As much as she disliked Charlotte, she had no wish to see her beaten. In truth, the duke did not appear to be the sort to raise his fists to his daughter. Surely, there would have been a sign such as Charlotte cringing or drawing back whenever he moved his arm.

"What business is it of yours, you –" He stopped himself when Nathaniel suddenly stepped between them, his expression ominous and forbidding. "Welles, I'll see to my daughter. There's no need for anyone to meddle. Now that the war's over, she and I will do a bit of traveling on the Continent. You'll like that, won't you Charlotte? Indeed, I think we'll leave first thing in the morning. You don't mind, do you?"

Nathaniel eased his stance and cast him a wry smile. "I'll get over the disappointment."

"Gad, what a mess," he muttered, turning to Poppy once the Winthrows had retired and they were alone. "The girl tried to ruin you and you still worried for her safety."

"The duke is a stern man. I didn't want him hitting her, although I don't think he ever has. I sincerely hope their trip to Europe will do her good."

He laughed softly and shook his head. "Poppy, not everyone is good."

She nodded. "I know. I see nothing but frustration and envy in her. And yet, she's the one who has been given every advantage in life."

"She isn't you, Poppy. She isn't kind or caring. Her heart isn't gentle and her touch isn't soothing." He took her back in his arms and kissed her gently. "I'll obtain the special license tomorrow. "How fast do you think Penelope and Lavinia can assemble a wedding celebration?"

She laughed heartily. "Your sister? She'd have us married this very night if it was left to her."

"And you?"

"I'd have us married this very night, as well. I love you, Nathaniel. I hope you don't mind my telling you that every day of your life."

"No, love. Don't mind at all."

Chapter Fourteen

"Two weddings in less than a month," Vicar Carstairs intoned, nodding to Nathaniel and casting an obviously wistful gaze at Poppy who looked radiant in her cream satin.

Nathaniel stood beside her before the altar, their wedding ceremony attended by family, friends, and the citizens of Wellesford who were all crowded in the church this morning.

He looked toward the pews with satisfaction, pleased to see Penelope and Lavinia seated in front. Beast, Goose, and Thad sat right behind them. Poppy's family was in attendance as well, her parents and sister, Violet, who looked upon Poppy in adoration. Her Aunt Sophie and Uncle John and their identical twins, Lily and Daffodil, were seated beside them.

To his surprise, Pip sat with the twins and Violet, the four of them with their heads bowed, looking in fascination at something in the boy's hands.

"His spider," Poppy said with a quiet laugh. "Some things never change."

When the ceremony started, he took Poppy's hands in his and held them as they exchanged vows. "Poppy," he said in an aching whisper, wondering how he would convey the breadth of his love for her. *Did she know? Could she feel it?* He'd lost his way after returning home from the Continent. He'd lost his heart. *The Book of Love* had set him back on his path home. That path led to Poppy. She was his home and hearth.

She'd always been there, waiting for him to find his way.

"Nathaniel, I'm so happy." Her eyes were bright and shimmering with love for him. No wiles, just open and honest feelings. She was too happy to mind when Pip dropped a spider onto her slice of wedding cake. "It's his way of welcoming me into the family."

After the festivities, they retired to Nathaniel's bedchamber, now theirs to share throughout their marriage. The guests had remained, and music and food continued to flow. He supposed they'd all go home once the food had all been eaten.

"It is a lovely party, Nathaniel. I'll have to thank Penelope and Lavinia for organizing it so beautifully."

"Plenty of time to let them know tomorrow." He took her into his arms.

She cast him one of her beautiful Poppy smiles. "Are you going to kiss me with conviction?"

He chuckled. "Yes, and leave your gown askew… for as long as you have it on, which won't be long."

He was true to his word, slipping the gown off her all the while he kissed her and stroked her and touched her in places that were a husband's right to claim.

When he'd filled her and felt her tremble with pleasure, heard her sighs and moans of ecstasy, he soared along with her, spilling his seed in her. He knew there would always be a part of him driven mindless by her body. But there was so much more to love than the physical urge to mate.

He watched her sleep in the quiet hours of the night.

He watched moonlight spill across her beautiful face.

He took her in his arms, glad that she was fast asleep, for his eyes began to fill with tears for all those lives he'd wished to save and couldn't. He understood now it wasn't his burden alone to handle.

He had Poppy to share it with.

He'd found his way home. She was his home.

"Nathaniel," Poppy said in a sleepy, contented whisper.

"Yes, love." He kissed her on the lips.

"I'm glad you looked at me and really saw me."

She was referring to *The Book of Love*. Yes, he'd finally looked and taken in her lavender scent and heard the lilting ripple of laughter in her voice, and tasted the sweetness of her lips.

But it was Poppy's touch that had soothed and healed him.

She appeared to be drifting off to sleep again, but she set her hand over his heart and murmured a yawning, "I love you, Nathaniel. Tomorrow night I'd like you to do to me what Lady Cordelia's count did to her on her Tuscan adventure."

"I love you, too," he whispered. "What did he do to her?"

They got no more sleep as Poppy began to show him.

Also by Meara Platt

FARTHINGALE SERIES
My Fair Lily
The Duke I'm Going To Marry
Rules For Reforming A Rake
A Midsummer's Kiss
The Viscount's Rose
Earl Of Hearts
The Viscount and the Vicar's Daughter
A Duke For Adela
If You Wished For Me
Never Dare A Duke
Capturing The Heart Of A Cameron

BOOK OF LOVE SERIES
The Look of Love
The Touch of Love
The Taste of Love
The Song of Love
The Scent of Love
The Kiss of Love
The Chance of Love
The Gift of Love
The Heart of Love
The Hope of Love (novella)
The Promise of Love
The Wonder of Love
The Journey of Love
The Treasure of Love
The Dance of Love
The Miracle of Love
The Dream of Love (novella)
The Remembrance of Love (novella)
All I Want For Christmas (novella)

MOONSTONE LANDING
Moonstone Landing (novella)
Moonstone Angel (novella)
The Moonstone Duke
The Moonstone Marquess
The Moonstone Major

DARK GARDENS SERIES
Garden of Shadows
Garden of Light
Garden of Dragons
Garden of Destiny
Garden of Angels

LYON'S DEN
The Lyon's Surprise
Kiss of the Lyon
Lyon in the Rough

THE BRAYDENS
A Match Made In Duty
Earl of Westcliff
Fortune's Dragon
Earl of Kinross
Earl of Alnwick
Aislin
Gennalyn
Pearls of Fire
A Rescued Heart
Tempting Taffy

DeWOLFE PACK ANGELS SERIES
Nobody's Angel
Kiss An Angel
Bhrodi's Angel

About the Author

Meara Platt is a *USA Today* bestselling author and an award winning, Amazon UK All-star. Her favorite place in all the world is England's Lake District, which may not come as a surprise, since many of her stories are set in that idyllic landscape, including her award-winning fantasy-romance Dark Gardens series. If you'd like to learn more about the ancient Fae prophecy that is about to unfold in the Dark Gardens series, as well as Meara's lighthearted, international bestselling Regency romances in the Farthingale series and Book of Love series, or her more emotional Braydens series, please visit her website at www.meara platt.com.

www.ingramcontent.com/pod-product-compliance
Lightning Source LLC
Chambersburg PA
CBHW070357200726
48294CB00003B/963

* 9 7 8 1 9 6 0 1 8 4 9 8 6 *